DEATH OVER DIVORCE

Also by Jerri Kay Lincoln:

Rutledge Historical Society Cozy Mysteries
Message for Murder
Death over Divorce
Kousins Kan't Kill
Rogues to Riches

Memoir
The Dog Who Rescued Me

Children's Books
Cooper's Smile
The Little Unicorn Who Could
Do Bears Poop in the Woods?
Can Pigs Fly?
Why Do Puppy Dogs Have Cold Noses?
The Invisible Lion
La Petite Licorne Qui Pouvait
Das Kleine Einhorn Was Es Kann
The Little Unicorn Who Could Coloring Book
Do Bears Poop in the Woods? Coloring Book

Cookbooks
Ten Delicious Dairy-Free Stevia-Sweetened Ice Cream
Recipes

Death over Divorce

Jerri Kay Lincoln

Ralston Store Publishing
P.O. Box 1684
Prescott, Arizona 86302

ISBN 978-1-938322-50-1

Professionally edited by:
Jennifer Hope
www.MesaVerdeMediaServices.com

The reader should note that the nutritional beliefs and food choices in this book are those of the characters and not necessarily those of the author or publisher.

Printed in the USA.

Dedicated to the sleuth in all of us.

CHAPTER ONE

IT WAS ANOTHER beautiful day in Rutledge, Arizona. It was a beautiful day even through the drizzle. All the days had been beautiful since I left my degenerate husband, Eddie—except the day I found the dead body of that poor woman on my first day of work at the Rutledge Historical Society. That was more of an ugly day. But it all got sorted out in the end, didn't it?

Looking into the backyard, I smiled. My dog, Bingo, was the second love of my life. And as I watched him, I couldn't help feeling grateful for the way everything had turned out. The house, the dog, and my son, Aiden. Although the adoption wasn't official yet, for Aiden and me, he was already my son.

I smiled as I watched Bingo pee on the yellow swing set that graced the backyard. No matter how many times Aiden tried to teach him, Bingo didn't understand that he wasn't supposed to pee on the swing set. It didn't hurt anything. But Aiden wanted him to stop, and Bingo wouldn't. I wasn't sure if Bingo did it on purpose or just because he could.

I opened the sliding glass door and Bingo ran inside.

Bingo, a Cavalier King Charles Spaniel, smiled up at me and shook, and when I leaned over with my arms open, he jumped into them. We rubbed our faces against each other, and I swear, it was like we were both purring. Oh wait, dogs and people don't purr, do they? Well, we both felt like we were purring, and that's all that mattered. Bingo was mostly black and white, but had tan eyebrows and a touch of tan on each cheek that made him look like he had rouge on.

As I walked by Aiden's room, his door was half closed as usual. I knocked softly. "Aiden, honey, time to get ready for school." Aiden was seven years old, and he was the first love of my life. Although I'd known him less than a year, my heart was his from the first day we met.

"Okay, Mom," he said in a soft voice trying to sound sleepy.

We had this routine, Aiden and I: he would keep his door half closed and pretend to be asleep in the mornings even though he was reading. I pretended not to know, and he pretended that he didn't know that I knew. It may sound confusing, but Aiden and I, we had it down pat. Bingo pushed open Aiden's door and jumped on the bed to reveal the last seconds of Aiden hiding the book under his covers. Again, I pretended not to see.

"Bingo! Bingo!" Aiden said as the dog jumped on his chest. It was a good thing Bingo didn't weigh that much —about fifteen pounds on a good day. Bingo barked happily in between licks of Aiden's face.

Aiden's room was all boy. We had bought the race car bed right before he moved in with me. It wasn't his first choice or his second or his third. When they didn't have his first choice, he got frustrated and said he didn't care what the bed looked like. His first choice was a bed that looked like a book, but unfortunately nothing like that existed. When he refused to choose any further, I bought this one because I thought it was cool, and I liked the color—a rich blue with black trim.

Next to the bed stood a tall floor lamp that had a light right at bed level. Aiden wanted that so he could read in bed. Except for a small desk in the corner with a computer on it, the rest of the room had bookcases in every available space. In case you're not getting the picture so far, do I need to explain that my son had a book addiction? Not such a bad thing, when you think about it.

Aiden, dressed in his Winnie the Pooh feet pajamas, strolled into the kitchen and sat down at the table. Bingo put his two front paws on Aiden's lap. It had taken awhile to teach Aiden *and* Bingo that it was a no-no for Bingo to be on Aiden's lap as he ate breakfast. Although I was lenient with Aiden, there were some things I wouldn't stand for. I loved Bingo, too, but he didn't belong sitting at the table when we ate. There was a breakfast bar between the kitchen and living room, but Aiden preferred sitting at the table for Bingo's sake. I didn't think it was something we needed to argue about. As long as Bingo was good—and he was—then I didn't care where Aiden chose to eat his breakfast.

"Eggs today?" I asked.

"No, not today."

"Oatmeal?"

"No."

"What do you want then?"

"Cereal and juice."

That's what he always wanted, and that's what I usually gave him. I put the cereal in a bowl, poured the milk into it, set it in front of Aiden, and glared at Bingo until he put his four feet on the floor. Then I poured the orange juice with pulp into a juice glass and gave it to Aiden. He taught me to drink orange juice with pulp. He said there were more vitamins in it, and he refused to drink any without pulp. So I learned to drink it that way, too.

After breakfast, as Aiden got dressed for school, I put the dishes into the dishwasher and cleaned up the kitchen. By the time I made his lunch, a peanut butter and jelly sandwich, a four-inch piece of cucumber, and two Oreo Double-Stuffs, he had his jacket and backpack on and was ready to go. Aiden put his arms out for me to inspect what he had on. He wore blue jeans with a Batman belt buckle that I had bought at a swap meet, a blue t-shirt that said "I am awesome!" on it, and his white Van's skate shoes with dogs printed all over them. With his blond hair and blue eyes, decorated with the longest eyelashes you've ever seen, Aiden was a really cute kid. And he was mine, so don't get any ideas.

I snapped the leash on Bingo, and the three of us traipsed outside. Looking back at the house, I smiled. It was *our* house. After Eddie let his and my house go into foreclosure, I had felt devastated over losing it, but now Aiden and I had this one, and Aiden was a much better companion than Eddie. And at seven years old, he was probably more mature, too. Our house was a gambrel— the kind of house that looked like a barn—complete with red paint and white trim. I loved it.

It had stopped drizzling, and the sky had cleared. After I buckled Aiden into the seat belt, Bingo jumped into the back with him, and then I climbed into the driver's seat. My new *used* Taurus—courtesy of my mother's attorneys doling out enough money to replace the falling-apart Karmann Ghia that I used to drive—was in great shape. It started right up, just like it should. I loved that car. As we drove toward the Rutledge Historical Society, we passed Martha and Hugo Goldstein. I gave them a brief honk of my horn, and Aiden pressed the button to roll down his window. "Hi, Grammy! Grampy!" he called.

They weren't really his grandmother and grandfather, but they had become his surrogate grandparents shortly after Aiden started living with me. I had been staying at their bed and breakfast at the time, and Aiden fit right in. We didn't stay long, though, before we moved into our own house.

After Hugo's heart attack, to encourage him to exercise more, Martha had persuaded him to walk her to work every day. So we now saw them most days on our way in to work and school. Martha was also my boss.

Two minutes later, we pulled into my parking space behind the Rutledge Historical Society. I never locked the car—not too many people did in Rutledge. Except during zucchini season, that is. As the joke goes, during zucchini season, you locked the doors to prevent people from putting zucchinis *into* your car.

The three of us walked toward the school, Aiden holding Bingo's leash, and Aiden and I holding hands. We didn't have to cross any streets to get to the elementary school which was on the next block over. It was because of that close proximity that Aiden and I had even met, those short months ago. As we approached the two-story red brick building, children and parents swarmed in front of it. And Pamela Reilly, the principal, stood at the top of the steps welcoming in children and parents alike. She wore a light and dark gray checked suit with dark gray shoes to match. Pamela, in her mid-thirties, was always the ultimate professional.

Aiden handed me the leash, reached up for a big hug, and said, "I love you, Mommy!" as he pranced off to play with his friends. My eyes blinked back tears as I watched him. My heart ached with all the love I had for that kid. When I looked up from watching him, I noticed that Pamela was trying to get my attention. It was almost time for school to begin, and the crowd around the stairs had thinned out. I walked up the stairs toward Pamela and smiled.

"So it's going well with Aiden?" she said and smiled back at me.

"Yes. Can you tell?"

She laughed. "Yes, I don't think there's any doubt."

"Pamela, I can't thank you enough for what you did." She had been instrumental in arranging Aiden's adoption for me. If it hadn't been for her, I don't know if it would have happened at all. Of course, my mother's attorneys had a hand in it, too, but that was a whole 'nother story.

"Oh! It was nothing. I can tell a *pair* when I see one." She looked at me seriously. "Listen, I know how much Aiden loves reading, and he's in the accelerated reading class now, but I wanted to ask you something. He's been helping the other remedial readers that he used to be in class with, and he's been quite successful. The teacher says Aiden has gained ground with these students that she hasn't been able to. I was wondering if you would mind if Aiden helped in remedial reading instead of being in the accelerated reading class, because honestly, Lorry, he's too advanced for that class, anyway."

"Would Aiden want to return to that remedial reading class?"

Pamela nodded. "He asked to. His teacher wasn't sure if she should let him or not, so she asked me. I told her to let him try it, and if I hadn't run into you today, I was going to call you."

"If Aiden wants to, and it makes him happy, then it's fine with me. He and I read together all the time, and he reads in bed, too. So he's getting plenty of his own reading in."

"Great! Thanks, Lorry!" Pamela briefly touched my shoulder, turned around, and disappeared into the school.

Bingo and I walked back down the stairs and trudged slowly back to the Rutledge Historical building. As I walked by my car, I noticed something in it. When I turned my head to see, it was that degenerate ex-husband of mine, Eddie Keeley, sleeping in my car with his head against the window. This was too much. I had to put a stop to it at once.

To be honest, I hadn't seen him in a couple of months. Shortly after I left him, he came to me begging for money, and I told him to get lost. He finally listened. So what in heaven's name was he doing sleeping in my car now?

I tapped on the window. He leaned so heavily on the window that I was afraid that if I opened the door, he would fall right out. My tapping didn't wake him, so I tapped louder. Still no response. If I tapped any harder, it would break my window, and I didn't want to do that. If I had to choose between breaking my car window or having Eddie fall out and break an arm, I would definitely choose him breaking his arm. The jerk. I loved

7

that car. It was just like my Taurus that Eddie had wrecked when we were married.

With my hand on the door, I was about to open it, when I heard a siren. Sirens are rare in Rutledge. No matter, I had to get the jerk out of my car. I opened the door and Eddie fell out onto the parking lot, just as the sheriff's car, with its lights flashing and its sirens blazing, pulled up behind my car. The sheriff's car distracted me, but as I glanced at Eddie lying on the ground, I saw something that I couldn't see while he was in the car. There was a red hole in his head and blood all over the left side of his shirt. He looked dead.

CHAPTER TWO

SHERIFF BILLY MADRIGAL walked toward me with one hand on his gun and the other hand pointed toward me. "Lorry Lockharte, don't move." Billy towered over me, and with the serious expression on his face, he looked quite intimidating.

"Billy, Eddie looks dead!"

"Get away from him, Lorry. Go on now. Step away and don't move."

It was only then that I noticed Billy's hand was on his gun, and he was *gripping* the gun like he was ready to draw it. My hands flew up over my head, except the hand holding Bingo's leash, which only went up about halfway. Bingo was a short dog. "Billy? You think *I* did this?"

"Lorry Lockharte, you have the right to remain silent. Anything you say may be used against you in a court of law. You have the right to—"

"You're reading me my *rights*? Come on, Billy!" I pleaded with him but kept my hands held high—at least one of them was held high, the other at half mast.

Billy stepped over to Eddie's body, and as he felt for a

pulse, he glanced at me. "I just got a call saying there was a murder taking place back here. And I drive up, and here you are, and your ex-husband Eddie is dead! What am I *supposed* to think?" Billy looked into my car that still had the door open. "And look at that." He pointed into the car.

There on the floor of the passenger side was a big gun. If I wasn't mistaken, it was the *smoking* gun. I had a bad feeling about this, and as much as I wanted to run away, I made my feet stay where they were. Who could run away in three-inch heels, anyway?

Billy keyed the microphone clipped to his chest. "Send me an ambulance to the back of the historical society building, call the medical examiner that we'll be delivering a body, and send the forensic team as well." He looked at me. "Lorry, Eddie was in your car and the gun is right there. I *have* to take you in." Then he finished reciting my rights to me.

I patiently waited until he finished, but my arms were getting tired. "Billy, come on. You know me. You know how much I hated the guy, but I wouldn't kill him—especially not in my own car. I'm not an idiot!"

"I don't know you *that* well, Lorry, and this looks bad. And you can put your arms down, just stay away from the gun."

Men! I swear they could be short-sighted twits sometimes. "Billy, I just dropped Aiden off at school. I was at home before that. You can ask Aiden."

"I'm not asking a six-year-old."

"He's seven, Billy. Remember? You went to his birthday party. You got him a Tonka truck and a book on whales."

"Yes, yes, just get in the back seat of my car, Lorry.

10

And I'll need to impound your car."

"You're impounding my *car*? Oh, come on, Billy!"

He put his hands on his hips and frowned at me. "Lorry, whether you killed him or not, I saw him fall out of *your* car. It doesn't look good."

I exhaled fiercely and glanced down at Eddie once more. That guy had caused me so much trouble in the past few years, and now even dead, he wouldn't let up. He was still giving me grief. Knowing Eddie, he probably planned it that way. "Hey, Billy." I pointed to Eddie's shirt. "It's hard to see through all the blood, but look at his shirt. It looks like he had been out in the rain. Aiden and I didn't even leave for school until after it stopped raining."

As I said the comment about the blood, I realized all that blood was grossing me out. My vision started narrowing, I got dizzy, and I was about to fall down right on top of Eddie's dead body when Billy must have caught me. I woke up when the ambulance arrived and the paramedics stuck smelling salts under my nose.

I was laid out like a corpse in the back of Billy's sheriff's car, with my legs hanging out the open door. The ceiling was gray, and something hard was sticking into my thigh. It turned out to be a seat belt attachment. Bingo was right below me licking my face. And I realized I was wearing my new beige skirt and that my legs were spread wide enough for anyone to see a complete show, not half a show, mind you, the *complete* show. I snapped them together so fast that my knees made a soft "whump" sound. Grimacing, I hoped that Billy didn't think it was a fart. But when I did it, one of my matching beige heels fell to the ground.

Billy picked it up. "Are you okay, Lorry?" He looked

down, concerned.

"I've had better days," I said as I struggled to sit up.

He gave me his hand to help me up. "I'm sorry, but I'm still going to have to take you in."

I frowned and shook my head. "Are you going to have to handcuff me too?"

The hint of a smile crossed his face, but he didn't let it show. "Only if you try to run off."

"Who's going to take care of Bingo?" At the mention of his name, Bingo raised up from the floor and tried to lick my face again.

"He can come with you for now until you're transferred to county."

CHAPTER THREE

COUNTY. BILLY DIDN'T mean county, he meant the jail at Coyote Moon. There are seventeen counties in Arizona. There used to be sixteen until West Rutledge turned itself into Coyote Moon—to match the casino built there—and voted to change the name of the county. That's when East Rutledge changed its name to Rutledge and became its own county. Rutledge County. Smallest county in Arizona. We didn't even have a jail—which was why he planned to transfer me to Coyote Moon.

Color me scared. I shuddered at the thought of being in the Coyote Moon jail. Coyote Moon was the city across the Rutledge River. Their jail was full of losers and degenerates. I supposed that all jails were, but Coyote Moon would be worse because of all the crimes and criminals related to gambling. And how do I know this? Because that scoundrel ex-husband of mine, now dead, had been in that jail. If the rest of the inmates were like him, and I suspected they were, then I didn't want to be there. Would Billy really send me there? I shook my head because I really didn't know. Here I was sitting in his patrol car, and I could barely believe that. The back seat was black, hard-molded plastic. There was a metal barrier between the front seat and the back seat. At seat-top level, the metal barrier turned to glass on one side, and a heavy metal screen on the passenger side. You could get the tips of your fingers through, but nothing else. I could see stuff in the front of the car, but wasn't interested enough to look. The whole situation was more than I could handle.

Patting the seat beside me, I invited Bingo up. He jumped into my arms and immediately began licking my face, which was exactly what I needed. At least somebody loved me and believed in me.

Billy hadn't closed the door to his car, so he must not have worried about me running away. One look at my heels would have told him that. I watched as they loaded Eddie, already in a body bag, into the ambulance. Then I watched as the forensic team—still looking twelve years old like the last time I had seen them in action several months ago—placed black fingerprint dust all over my car, the gun, and the general area. When they finished that, Billy directed them to drive my car into the impounding area behind the tall chain-link fence at the sheriff's station.

Billy walked over to the car and looked in at me. "You all set?"

"Not really, Billy. I can't believe you're doing this."

He shrugged and reached in to pet Bingo, but Bingo, who normally loved Billy, bared his teeth at him. Billy shrugged again and closed the door. Then he climbed into the front seat and started the car. On the sixty-second drive to the sheriff's station, we didn't speak. I was too angry, and Billy was probably distracted. He parked and then walked around and opened the door for me and Bingo. Smart man didn't try to pet Bingo again. I was hoping that Bingo would lift his leg on Billy's shoe, but no such luck. Billy had me walk in front of him, but he had one hand tight around my upper arm. "Hey," I told him. "Don't squeeze so hard, you'll make wrinkles that are tough to get out." He loosened up, but not much. It was a new blouse to match the beige skirt. Beige and white stripe. Very stylish. Billy opened the sheriff's station door as if it was made from cardboard. Last time I opened that door, it was so heavy that I had to use both hands. Color me impressed.

Stopping at the reception area, he leaned in. "Hey, bring me a GSR kit." Then he gently pushed me away from him, looked me up and down, and leaned back into the window. "Make it two." We walked into the back room, which was a hallway, and turned left. Billy opened the door for me and motioned me to enter. When I stepped in, I recognized the place from when I was fingerprinted here several months ago. The same white walls with industrial carpeting and the tall artificial plant wilting in the corner. It still needed dusting. Billy pointed toward the table and chairs. "Sit there and don't move. I'll be right back."

I wanted to make some smart-aleck comment, but being in a sheriff's station for a crime you didn't commit can sober a person up pretty quickly. Five minutes later Billy returned, carrying two plastic bags filled with some kind of objects, and wearing a disposable white apron.

Even feeling sober, I couldn't pass this one up. "Billy! You're cooking me dinner? Awesome! Here I thought you were going to fingerprint me."

He frowned and exhaled hard through his nose. "I'm sorry about this, Lorry, but it has to be done. And I'm not fingerprinting you. Remember? You did that a few months ago."

I nodded. "Yes, I remember. So if not fingerprinting, what are you going to do?" I eyed the contents of the bags suspiciously. "You're not going to take my blood, are you? For DNA or something?" Before he answered, I realized that my morning coffee was pressing to be released. "Billy, can I use the restroom? I really need to go."

He sat at the table opposite me and spread out a large tissue tablecloth. "No, Lorry, you have to wait until I administer a GSR test."

I crossed my legs tightly together. "What's a GSR test and why do I need one?"

"Gunshot residue. To see if you fired the gun." He opened one of the plastic bags, pulled out a pair of gloves, and put them on.

"I told you I didn't fire any gun! I've never seen that gun before. In fact, I've *never* shot a gun!"

Billy frowned again. "This test will verify that. Hopefully." He reached into the bag and pulled something else out. "Put your right hand on the table in front of me." I did as he said, and he applied an adhesive strip on it and then placed the strip into a small bottle. "Turn your hand over." He did the same to my palm. Then he did both sides of the left hand. Sealing the first bag, he pulled the second bag out and opened it.

"What's the second bag for? My feet?"

"No, Lorry, not your feet. Would you like to go in the other room and remove your clothing, or can we do it here?"

Sheriff Billy Madrigal was six feet four inches tall, broad at the shoulder and narrow at the hip (just like that old cowboy song), and filled out his dark brown sheriff's slacks nicely—front and back—if you get my drift. His outfit was complete with a light brown shirt, bolo tie sporting a Native American thunderbird in a turquoise inlay, and his signature Smokey Bear hat. I had always liked Billy, and I had been hoping that someday he would ask me to remove my clothing, but not at the sheriff's station while considered a suspect. Looking into his eyes, I scrunched my eyes at him. "Well, are you going to touch my boobs with that?" How do people see out of tightly scrunched eyes, anyway?

Billy closed his eyes and shook his head. "No, Lorry. I am not going to touch your boobs. I've never seen even trick shooters shoot a gun with their boobs. Just some areas on your clothing."

I pulled my hand away. "That stuff won't stain, will it? This blouse is new."

"And it's very pretty." He nodded his head. "But it won't stain. No."

I put my arms back out as he directed. He did two places on both sleeves, and then two places on my skirt. My blouse was tucked in. Although I'm pudgy, I liked the look of a tucked-in blouse better. Besides, you're not going to hide this pudge under a loose-fitting blouse. Everybody knows what's underneath, anyway, so why hide it?

When Billy finished and everything was back in the plastic bags, he took off the apron, pulled the tissue off the table, and stood up. "Okay, thanks, Lorry. Now I'm going to put you into the holding cell."

"So how long will this test take to clear me? Are you

going to run it right now?"

"It has to go to the forensic laboratory in Coyote Moon. They'll put it though a SEM. We don't have that kind of equipment here."

"What's a sem?"

"Scanning electron microscope." He opened the door to usher me out. "Down this hallway here." Opening another door, he escorted me inside. "Sorry about the accommodations." The room, lined with concrete blocks, had a straight chair in one corner and a ten gallon bucket with a fake toilet seat on top of it in the other corner.

I took one look and freaked out. "I can't pee there! Where am I going to wash my hands?"

"Lorry." His voice was low and annoyed.

"Come on, Billy. I didn't kill Eddie! The least you can do after these humiliations is let me use your toilet! Come on!"

"All right! Come down here." He marched me down the hallway to a door with a sign in front of it that showed a man and a woman on it. "Hurry up. I'm waiting right here."

"What if I have to—oh, forget it. I'll be right out." Bingo stepped in before me, and I closed and locked the door. The bathroom was small, but clean. A tile floor and light brown walls completed the decor. A few minutes later, after washing my hands with soap, Bingo and I stepped out to a waiting Billy. I should have left the water running. "Thank you. I appreciate your hospitality."

He led me back to the holding cell. "I'll call Petra and let her know you won't be in today." Then I heard the deadbolt lock behind him.

CHAPTER FOUR

YOU CAN'T IMAGINE what it feels like to be trapped in a ten by ten concrete room with no windows, a locked door, one chair, and a bucket with a makeshift toilet seat on it. Until Billy locked the door, I didn't believe he would lock me up. I sat in the chair, and Bingo jumped into my lap. Tears streamed down my face. If Bingo hadn't been there with me, I think I might have tried to hang myself by my shoelaces. But heels don't usually come with shoelaces, so I would have had to get creative. My bra? Whatever.

Bingo *was* with me, and as he sat on my lap, he licked my tears away, which made me smile. If you can sit in a cramped room like that and smile, you aren't as bad off as you think you are. But if I got sent to county, then it would be bad. There would be no Bingo there, and I've heard the stories of what happens in women's prisons, and I did not want any part of that. Plus, I was innocent! Leave it to Eddie to get me blamed for his murder. It would be just like him to plan something like that just to get back at me.

That was it! Eddie had climbed into my car, blown

himself away, and made it look like I did it! That degenerate jerk was trying to get back at me for not giving him any money. I'd bet anything that Eddie's own fingerprints were on the gun that was on the floor of my car.

My car! My poor car! It was impounded. When would I see it again? What would they do to it? Maybe it hadn't been such a good idea to get a car exactly like the car that Eddie wrecked. Would that be bad karma? No, I think it would be more like following a trend. Eddie had wrecked the first Taurus, and the second Taurus was involved in Eddie's murder. I should probably consider another kind of car.

I hugged Bingo and wondered what would happen if I got sent to county. What would happen to Aiden? The thought panicked me, and I had to stand up and walk around to shake off the anxiety. His adoption wasn't final yet. Would he be put back in the system—go back into foster care? I sat down, tried to calm myself, and then stood back up and walked around. Then I repeated the process again and again. Aiden! What would happen to Aiden?

Forcing myself to sit down, I began breathing deeply and concentrating on Aiden feeling safe and me feeling calm. Instead of thinking about the worst thing that could happen, think about the best. Me home tonight cooking dinner for Aiden. Me hugging Aiden. Aiden and I reading together before bedtime. The good thoughts calmed me more than I thought they would.

Taking a deep breath, I looked at my watch and sighed. It had been an hour and a half since I discovered Eddie's body, and twenty minutes since I had been locked in this concrete room. How long would I have to stay here?

There was a knock on the door, Bingo barked, and the door opened. Billy stepped aside to let another man walk in beside him. "Lorry Lockharte, meet your lawyer. Bryan O'Keefe."

Bryan O'Keefe wore an expensive suit, with a dark blue tie, and mirror-finish shoes. I could have applied my makeup with the reflection in those shoes. He was tall with black hair cut short and piercing dark brown eyes. He looked uptight and a little aggressive. The perfect lawyer.

Standing up to walk forward and shake Mr. O'Keefe's hand, I asked Billy, "How did that happen?"

Billy shrugged. "Petra must have called someone." Then he looked at *my* lawyer. "Mr. O'Keefe, did you want to use the interrogation room?"

Bryan O'Keefe turned. "No. But can I have another chair in here, please?"

"Yeah, sure." Billy disappeared momentarily and then returned with a second chair. He winked at me without smiling and then closed the door behind him. I returned to my seat.

Bryan O'Keefe pulled the chair opposite mine and sat down. "Your mother's attorneys sent me. I'm from Flagstaff."

"Thank you for coming, Bryan." As he settled into his chair, something occurred to me. "You mean Petra didn't call you?"

"No. As I said, your mother's attorneys." He looked around the concrete room and wrinkled his nose when he saw the ten gallon bucket.

"It's empty." At least I hoped it was. I noticed now that it had a plastic liner in it. The plastic stuck out the

21

sides under the toilet seat. "Bryan, I didn't kill Eddie. I hated him enough to kill him, but I didn't kill him."

He looked at me and narrowed his eyes. "*Never* say that again—about hating him enough to kill him. Someone hears you say something like that, and it could hang you. Literally. And I know you didn't."

"Yeah, whatever, but I *can* say that I'd choose death over divorce any day. It's cheaper and way less trouble."

"Lorry," his voice was low and sober, "look around you. See this concrete cell that you're in? If you got convicted of his murder, it would be a lot *more* trouble and a *lot* more expensive. I'm serious about this, Lorry. You cannot go around saying that you're glad your *estranged* husband, who was found dead in *your* car, is dead. That's enough for some people to doubt your innocence. And you can't afford that."

I glanced around and nodded. "Yeah, you're right. After my morning, I'm not straight in the head. What did you mean that you know I didn't kill Eddie?"

He shuffled through his briefcase and pulled out some papers. "Eight A.M. Let the dog out. 8:10 Wake the boy. 8:15 Serve breakfast. 8:30 Wash dishes and make lunch while son gets dressed. 8:45 Leave for work and school. 8:47 Arrive at Rutledge Historical Society. 8:48 Walk son to school and talk to principal. 9:05 Arrive back at Historical Society and find body." He looked up. "There was no way you could have done it."

My mouth hung open wide enough to catch a dozen flies, maybe two dozen. "You've been following me."

He nodded and said, "Someone has. Not me." Mr. O'Keefe was a man of few words.

"I wondered how the attorneys had known I was divorcing Eddie, had known about the adoption, had known so many things about me." I shook my head. "That clears up *that* mystery." It had been something I had puzzled over ever since the first check for five hundred dollars arrived from my mother's attorneys. When she died several years previously, they had told me that she had donated all of her money to charity and had not left me a single cent.

"According to your file, and there is no reason to keep it from you at this point, your mother didn't want you to know that she would be leaving you *any* money—as long as you stayed with Edward Keeley. She feared that he would arrange a devious scheme to get the money anyway."

"She knew him well. That's *exactly* what he would have done had he known about the money. And stupid me would have willingly gone along with it."

Bryan nodded. "Now that Eddie is dead, the full sum of money will be coming to you. There is a letter messengered to you right now advising you of that." He shook his head. "Unfortunately, that presents us with other difficulties. It will look like you already knew that and that's why you killed him."

"But I didn't kill him!" I protested.

"I know that and you know that. But Billy boy the sheriff does not, and right now, *he's* who counts. It depends how adamant he is about keeping you here."

Without thinking, I spoke up for Billy. "Don't call him Billy boy. He's my friend."

"Not much of a friend if he threw you in this joint." He cast his eyes around the small room, and they again landed on the makeshift toilet in the corner.

I frowned. That part was true enough. Billy should have believed me. Why didn't he? We had gotten along so well in the past few months, and I thought he was ready to ask me out on a date. Instead, he threw me in jail. What kind of friend was that? Apparently, I still had bad taste in men. Not much of a surprise, I suppose. Sighing, I said, "You're right about that."

"It would have been wiser of the attorneys to hold the letter until the murder had been solved, but your mother had left strict instructions that upon Edward Keeley's death, you were to be informed *immediately*."

"The attorneys can't think for themselves?" I said, a touch more irritably than I felt.

Bryan shook his head. "No offense, Lorry, but rumor has it that your mother was a tyrant."

Laughing, I said, "They got that right! She was! But what did they think? That she would come back from the grave and haunt them if they didn't follow her instructions?"

Bingo jumped into my lap at that moment, and I stroked him. What a strange provision to put in the will. Why would my mother even *think* that Eddie might die? He was only thirty-five years old. Everything surrounding Eddie's death had been weird. And now this.

CHAPTER FIVE

SOMEONE KNOCKED ON the door. It opened, and Billy stuck his head in. "Mr. O'Keefe, would you give me permission to take a DNA sample from your client?"

Before Bryan could even answer, I stood up. "His client says yes! Anything to prove my innocence!"

"Yes, it's all right with me," said Bryan.

"Wait here, I'll be right back." Billy closed the door, but I didn't hear the deadbolt slide into place. He returned with a plastic bag in his hand and walked toward me. Opening the bag, he pulled out what looked like a long Q-tip and said, "Open up." Why is it when someone tells you to open up, they open *their* mouth? Do they think you don't know what they mean? Billy had fillings in his back two bottom molars. He stuck the Q-tip into my mouth gently scraping the inside of my cheek. Then he placed it into a test tube and sealed the lid. I closed my mouth, and he closed his. "All done."

"What's this about, Sheriff Madrigal?" asked Bryan.

"Apparently, Eddie Keeley had sex shortly before he was killed."

My hands on my hips, I spat out, "And you think I—"

But I didn't get to finish because Bryan interrupted me.

"Well, then, wouldn't it be a good idea if she had a rape kit done on her?"

Billy looked down and put his hands in his pockets. He looked like an embarrassed little boy. "Well, I, uh—"

"Arrange it!" said Bryan.

"No!" I said. "I don't want a rape kit! I haven't had sex in—"

"It doesn't matter how long ago you had sex, Lorry," said Bryan. "It only matters that it wasn't this morning with Eddie."

"But I don't want a rape kit."

This time Billy turned toward me. With one hand still in his pocket, he put the other hand on my shoulder. "Lorry, if you do this, it will eliminate you as a suspect. That's what you want, isn't it?"

"Will I still have to go to county?" I said in a voice so small that I didn't even recognize it as my own.

Billy hesitated, and Bryan spoke up. "Sheriff Madrigal, I have a private investigator's report right here showing exactly what Ms. Lockharte was doing this morning." Bryan reached into his briefcase. Made of a deep reddish leather, it probably cost more than my car.

Billy shook his head. "No need to see it. No, Lorry, you don't have to go to county. I'll formally release you after you, um, finish."

The sigh that escaped my lips was felt all the way down to my toes. Just knowing that I wouldn't have to go to county was a huge relief.

"I'll escort you down there," said Billy. "They can do it at Urgent Care down the street. No need to go to the hospital in Coyote Moon."

"How about if *I* escort her down there?" asked Bryan.

Billy nodded. "Yes, that would be all right."

"And will she need to return here afterward, or can she go on her way?"

"She can go on her way." Billy looked at me with remorse in his eyes. "I'm sorry about this, Lorry, but I had to be sure."

I looked at him, shrugged, and shook my head. What he did to me was uncalled for, and I still felt angry about it. Billy held open the door, and Bryan and I and Bingo walked out of the holding cell.

Wanting to get out of the building and away from the thought of the cement holding cell, Bingo and I hurried to the outside door, but Bryan called me back to the receptionist. "Let's get your belongings before we go."

"What belongings?"

Bryan looked at me like I was nuts. "What he took from you when he put you in the cell."

"He didn't take anything from me." I looked down. "Bingo's right here." It was then that I realized that I had left my purse in the car. I always left it in the unlocked car while I walked Aiden to school. And I usually forgot to get it out of the car when I went in to work. It would sometimes be hours later when I realized it and walked out to get it. Today I had forgotten about it completely. "Uh oh. I left my purse in the car."

"Oh" said a voice from behind the receptionist. "It's right here. I'll bring it out." Billy came out of the back with the purse in his hand. It looked as if he had rifled through it. "I had to do the GSR test inside the purse, but everything is still there." He handed me the purse.

I grabbed it out of his hand and turned to go. "Whatever!"

"And I found this inside." Billy held up a handful of

27

bullets in a plastic bag with a zipper top.

"Billy, I don't even own a gun!"

"These bullets fit the gun left in the car with Eddie."

"Are there any fingerprints on them?" asked Bryan.

"None at all."

"Figures." Bryan held the door open for me, and we walked outside.

I took a deep breath of fresh air and smiled. "Smell that?" I asked.

Bryan sniffed the air. He crinkled his nose thinking it was something bad. "What?"

"The sweet smell of freedom."

CHAPTER SIX

THE SHERIFF'S STATION was on Main Street, and so was the Urgent Care Clinic. Bryan, Bingo, and I walked across the street and the short way down the block. It was next to the Town Offices, which I thought was smart. Anyone who fainted or had a heart attack from all the bureaucracy at the Town Offices only had a short way to go to a doctor. Martha worked at the Town Offices, and although I never had issues there, I had heard of people who did.

The Urgent Care Clinic was another of the newer buildings in Rutledge made of concrete with a green trim. There were two doors to get into the building, which was stupid. The two doors were five feet apart and kitty-corner from each other. They both led into a small entryway with another door.

Bryan held the outside door open for me, I opened the second door for myself, and Bingo and I walked in. Although I saw the sign that said dogs not permitted inside, I had found that if you acted like you belonged there, then often, you could get away with it. There were also those people who had fake therapy dog vests for their dogs, so they could take them places. I'd never do that. But I had no problem acting like I belonged there.

When you walked in, there were dual waiting areas, one to the left and one to the right, and a right-angled reception desk straight ahead servicing both waiting areas. I always thought maybe the building was originally designed for an animal hospital, dogs on the right, cats on the left, because there was no apparent reason for the separation. Both sections had a large television screen hanging from the ceiling that continuously played a medical infomercial trying to get you interested in buying more pharmaceuticals. Between that and the other office accoutrements including a drug-oriented calendar, drug-oriented business card holders, drug-oriented pens, and a drug-oriented clock, every time I walked in the place, I began to feel sick. The sooner I got out of there, the better.

I proceeded to the reception area and found that an old high school chum greeted me. Candy Apple Howe had on white jeans and a blue and white striped blouse. Her hair had been cut short, but it suited her. "Hi, Lorry! I heard you were back in town! We got a call from Sheriff Billy, and you'll be seeing Dr. Anderson. He's with a patient right now, but will be with you shortly. We'll put you in a room now, and you can get ready." She leaned forward with a concerned look on her face. "Are you okay?" she said barely above a whisper.

Sighing, I shook my head. This whole episode was getting so tiring already. Leave it to Eddie to haunt me even when he was dead. "I wasn't raped. This is about something else."

"But they said it was a rape kit."

I nodded. "Long story, Candy. Where do I go?"

Bryan stepped up beside me. "How about if I take your dog?"

"Yes, that's a good idea," said Candy. "He shouldn't be in the examining room."

I handed Bingo to Bryan and patted him on the head —Bingo, not Bryan—and told him to be a good boy. "Hopefully I won't be too long. Thanks for taking him." Then the door opened, and Candy motioned me inside.

She showed me the paper gown to put on and left the room without any more conversation, which made me very happy. This whole situation was ugly enough without having to explain it to someone you hadn't seen in more than ten years.

Candy Apple obtained that nickname in high school after a traveling carnival came to town. She had eaten too many candy apples—on a dare—and then gone on the Ferris wheel, which was not such a good idea. Let's say that the people on that Ferris wheel got more than they had expected. And Candice "Candy" Howe was stuck with the nickname Candy Apple Howe through the rest of high school. As nicknames go, it wasn't a particular bad one, just one laden with bad memories.

I had gotten my clothes off and the paper gown on and was sitting on the edge of the examining table when Dr. Anderson walked in. He was tall and good looking— exactly the kind of doctor you don't want during this kind of procedure. He also looked like he had just gotten out of medical school. I hoped that he knew what he was doing so I wouldn't have to go through this twice.

"Lorry Lockharte? I'm Dr. Anderson. I understand that you have not actually been raped, but the sheriff is requesting this for DNA purposes." He shook my hand.

"Yes, that's all true. I'm not happy about it, but the

sooner I can get past this, the sooner I can move on."

"Don't worry." He patted me on the shoulder. "It shouldn't take long." He pressed a button on the intercom and then washed his hands in the sink.

When I had come into the room, I noticed there was the ubiquitous metal tray with a speculum and a plastic bag on it. I had seen enough plastic bags with invasive instruments inside them, that day, to last me for the next year. The nurse came in and told me to lie down and scoot forward. She put my feet in the stirrups and shined a light down there where the sun don't shine.

The doctor sat on a swivel chair in front of said places. Besides giving me the usual play-by-play of what he was doing, he carried on an inane conversation meant to put me at ease. Said conversation was on the order of, "Hey, how 'bout them Dodgers?" Gratefully, in a moment it was over. The conversation and the procedure.

"I'll get this over to the sheriff right away," said Dr. Handsome, as he walked to the sink to wash his hands again.

"Thanks." It's difficult to maintain your dignity when you're lying there with your legs spread and a bright light shining on your private parts. Although the light was off, I could still feel the heat on my skin. I was just happy that he hadn't said anything like, "It's obvious that *you* haven't had sex in a long time." I didn't need the reminder.

CHAPTER SEVEN

AFTER GETTING DRESSED and saying goodbye to Candy Apple Howe, I walked out to where Bryan and Bingo were waiting. Bingo greeted me like we had been separated for years. It wasn't that long ago that I *hadn't* seen him for years, and since he was back, he had developed a minor case of separation anxiety. Of course, so had I. I'm not sure who had caught it from whom. I tried to keep him with me all the time now. Luckily, Martha allowed me to take him to work with me every day.

"Where would you like me to take you? I could take you to your cousin's house, or I can take you to Coyote Moon to buy a new car."

"Buy a new car? Why?"

"They'll be keeping your old car in impound for a while, and it might carry bad memories for you. Your mother's attorneys have instructed me to buy you another car."

"Buy me another car? Wow." Eddie's death was getting more palatable by the instant. And I was well aware that would make me look even more guilty. "If my cousin is home, I'd like to go there. Too much excitement for one day already. I don't think I could concentrate on getting a car right now." I wasn't even going to ask how he knew about my cousin. Apparently my mother's attorneys knew everything about me including how often I popped a pimple. It took small town living to a whole new level of non-privacy. Reaching into my purse, I pulled out my cell phone and called my cousin Kasey. Although I had called her Cruella DeVille since first grade when she stole my boyfriend away, it had been more than twenty-five years since then, so I let wisdom triumph over wit and had let that go.

"Lorry! Are you all right? I heard about Eddie! And you found him! Wow! Aiden wasn't there with you, was he? Do you need—"

"Kasey! Stop for a second! Would you mind if I came over right now?" Kasey sometimes—no, usually—talked more than she listened. She had a good heart, but a big mouth.

"Yes! Yes, of course! Come now! I'll be—"

"Okay, see you soon. Bye!" I hung up before she could go on. "I'm not sure if it's a good idea for me to go over there or not. My nerves are already shot as it is."

"I'm sure it will be fine. Here's my car." He was parked in front of the sheriff's station, and he opened the passenger door for me and Bingo. We got in. It was a white Buick with a white leather interior. I hoped that Bingo wouldn't shed on the fancy white seats, but whatever. Dogs will be dogs, and I couldn't control where his fur would fall. But, Bryan, being a gentleman, didn't seem to care.

He drove me straight over to Kasey's house without me having to give him any directions. When he stopped in front, he put the car in park and turned to me. "Lorry, if you would like me to purchase a new car *for* you, I would be happy to do it. Tell me exactly what you want, and I will arrange it."

I shrugged my shoulders and shook my head. "I'm so overwhelmed right now, Bryan, I have no idea what I would want."

"Think about it. And take this." He handed me a business card. "If you need anything or have any more trouble from Billy boy, let me know. I'll take care of it."

"Thank you." I opened the door, Bingo jumped out, and I followed. This time I wasn't going to defend Billy.

"I'll be in touch, Lorry," said Bryan before I had a chance to close the door.

Bingo and I stood there as Bryan drove away. My mother, dead and buried for years now, had finally come through for me. Since I had left Eddie, I had gotten a new car—and now would be getting another one—a new house, help with Aiden's adoption, and now help through the ordeals of being accused of murder.

And all that was after Mother's attorneys had informed me that she had left me nothing and given all her money to charity. It didn't matter. It hadn't been true, and now I was receiving the benefits I had once hoped to get. And with Eddie gone, it wouldn't even be doled out any more—I would get the rest of her money. And she had a ton. Lost in these thoughts, I was half surprised when Kasey called to me from her front door.

"Lorry! Are you okay?" She stood there holding her six-month-old son, Zandor—named after a Weather Channel storm that had never happened.

I walked up to her, and she wrapped her arms around me, squishing my face against Zandor's. His face was soft and comforting, and he didn't seem to mind. "I'm okay now, Kasey, I'm okay now."

Standing aside so we could walk into her house, she said something that made me want to start calling her Cruella DeVille again. "Lorry, I know how much you hated Eddie." She looked at me with wide-eyed wonder and whispered the rest. "So, did you do it?"

CHAPTER EIGHT

I PUT MY hands on my hips and stared at her. "Kasey! You really believe I could do such a thing? No! Of course I didn't kill that scumbag Eddie!" As I was about to tell her that I wanted to do it, I remembered what Bryan had said about not saying anything like that, so I kept quiet.

Kasey invited me into her living room. I sat down and took the leash off Bingo. Zandor was getting fussy, so Kasey bared her breast and started feeding him. While she settled him in, I looked around the room. Kasey and her husband, John, the high school principal, lived in a large four-bedroom Cape Cod home. The lawn and landscaping were perfect. Inside was a different story. Their furniture had once been nice, but had borne the brunt of their tomboy daughter, Lily. She was a sweet kid, but hard on the furniture and everything else.

The light sage green walls of their living room were decorated by a child's scrawl, as was the beautiful autumn wallpaper in the dining room. I even recognized a picture in back of the couch drawn by Aiden. Kasey and John didn't believe in disciplining their children, so

Lily, and anyone she invited over, had free run of the place. Their eighty-inch large-screen television had already been replaced three times because of balls thrown in the den. One of those three times, Aiden did it. But I never offered to pay, because I would never have allowed him to throw the ball in the house anyway. Since Kasey and John allow it, then they suffer the consequences. It sounds hard of me, but you have to draw the line somewhere.

Kasey looked up from Zandor. "So? Tell me everything."

And I did. Starting from seeing Eddie "sleeping" in the car, to him falling out of the car with a bullet in his head, to suffering the humiliation of not only being in that concrete holding cell but having to endure the rape kit, and finally about Bryan—sent by my mother's attorneys—offering to buy me a new car. I had never heard Kasey stay quiet for so long. Apparently, she could be a good listener if she wanted to. Telling the story had gotten me all riled up again, so I started pacing the room, back and forth in front of Kasey. Although Bingo was off leash, he followed me across the floor.

"Come on, Lorry, you'll wear a hole in the carpeting!"

I looked down at the carpeting. Except for the multitude of stains, the deep plush carpeting could have been brand new. Side-stepping past a rather large grape juice stain, I made my way back to the couch with Bingo following. But the grape juice had reminded me of all the blood on Eddie, so I sank into the couch cushions, leaned forward, and put my head between my knees. Breathing as deeply as I could, I made the moment pass.

It would be a long time before I got that vision of Eddie out of my head. It was bad enough to visualize him before, but now—that miserable Eddie always trying to make me miserable right along with him. Misery loves company was Eddie's motto. When he won at cards, he'd bring me flowers or gifts, and then sneak out to one of his girlfriends to celebrate, expecting the gift to appease me. And I always took him back.

Kasey struggled to get up, with Zandor holding on. "Lorry! Are you all right?"

I picked up my head, but continued the deep breathing. "I was just thinking of all that blood on Eddie." Shivering, I continued, "It was gruesome, that's all. And I hate having that image come into my mind."

"Eddie always knew how to get to you."

"Yeah, even in death, he doesn't let up." Leaning forward, I whispered, "I'm glad he's dead! But don't tell anyone I said that. Come on, Kasey, I'm counting on you." The words had just slipped out, and as soon as I said them, I knew it was a mistake. It wasn't only that Bryan had warned me against it. It was that Kasey had the biggest mouth in town, and everyone who came into the Rutledge Koffee Korner Kafe coffee shop where she worked was her audience. "Please, Kasey, don't say anything to anyone."

"No, no, of course I won't."

She looked so sincere when she said it. Kasey was like a talking kleptomaniac: she had a need to talk and she couldn't help herself. Apparently it ran in the family, because I had just told her exactly what Bryan told me not to. Too late now.

"Let's talk about what kind of car you're going to get. Will it be another Taurus? John and I have been talking about getting a car and were thinking about a Toyota RAV4, but John thought it might be too small if we have any more children. Because we've been talking about that, too!" She smiled at me conspiratorially. "He wants to have more, and I don't—at least not right now." Laughing, she put her hands over Zandor's ears and said quietly, "I'm taking birth control pills, but John doesn't know."

Then she took her hands away. She did that because she probably didn't want Zandor—who couldn't talk yet —telling her husband what she was doing. Then I wondered if everyone at the Koffee Korner knew she was taking birth control pills and if John, her husband, was the only one who didn't know.

CHAPTER NINE

AS I SAT there listening to Kasey, I noticed what she was wearing. Normally, I saw her while she was working and dressed in her yellow waitress uniform that made her look like a canary. Today, she wore a white blouse with baby spit all over it, and faded yellow capris—she must really be into yellow—with one pocket half torn off. It was probably more damage from Lily. And she was barefoot. One foot had red nails, and half the nails on the other foot were red. She must have been interrupted in the middle and forgotten to finish. Kasey wasn't a clothes hound like I was. I could say that having a baby around might change your perspective on clothes, but Kasey hadn't been into clothes even in high school. She and I were cousins, but nothing alike.

Kasey rattled on and on about the car she and John were going to buy, and I got more and more antsy. I had probably stopped listening to her prattle several cars earlier when I suddenly jumped to my feet and started pacing again.

"What's wrong, Lorry? Did you decide which car you wanted to buy?"

Shaking my head, I said, "No, yes, a RAV4 sounds great. I'm just nervous. I still can't believe this happened and I'm a suspect. What will happen to Aiden? Would they stop the adoption proceedings if this gets out?"

"Well, he can always come and live here with us. He and Lily love each other."

That part was true, but I looked around the room—at the scribbled-on walls and the juice-stained carpet—and didn't think I wanted Aiden living here full time. I only had to hope everything got sorted out in time. Then I realized Aiden needed to be picked up from school, and I didn't have a car. "Aiden!" I looked at my watch and relaxed when I realized he had several hours to go.

When Kasey finished feeding Zandor, she stood up. "Lorry, I know what you need to clear your head and calm you down. Can you put water in the tea kettle while I put him down for a nap?" She headed upstairs before I even answered.

How could I think about tea at a time like this? My life was at stake! Aiden's life was at stake! What would become of him if I went to jail? Besides, I didn't even like tea. But dutifully, I rose from my seat and walked into the kitchen. As I stood there waiting for the water to fill up the tea kettle, I couldn't get Eddie out of my mind. Then my mind moved on to that concrete holding cell I was in. It was terrible. Then Bryan and the rape kit and — The water ran out of the top of the tea kettle, so I shut the water off and poured some out. Moving over to the stove, I set the tea kettle on the front burner as images from my morning tortured me.

I began pacing again, back and forth, back and forth, with Bingo at my heels. Poor boy, he kept looking up at me. He probably thought his mother had gone crazy. But

I couldn't help myself. It was like I had all this pent-up energy, and I had to walk it off or else I might burst into flames.

Kasey came down then and watched as I paraded back and forth. "Now you're going to wear a hole in the linoleum! Here, let me get you some tea." Walking over to the stove, she reached for the kettle, and then quickly touched it with the tips of her fingers. "Lorry! You didn't turn it on! You *are* distracted!" She turned on the burner and reseated the tea kettle. "Sit down. Let me massage your shoulders. That should help. And this tea will fix everything."

"Yeah, right," I said as I slid into the chair. "What is it? Marijuana tea? I've heard that fixes everything. A real panacea, I've heard. No thank you." Kasey pressed her thumbs into the back of my neck, and it felt good. "Ooohhhh. Don't stop."

"Good, I'm glad you're finally relaxing. No, it's not marijuana tea, silly! It's called Yerba Mate, and it's from South America. It will help to clear your mind."

Kasey continued massaging my back, and it was working. All I could croak out was, "I don't like tea. I'm not a tea drinker."

Without stopping the massage, Kasey answered, "You'll drink this tea. It's good for you. And you'll thank me for it later."

Between moans, I said, "Yeah, right. Thank you. Yeah."

Kasey stopped massaging when the tea kettle whistled. I felt so relaxed that I couldn't move. She took out two cups, opened a container, pulled out some tea leaves, ran them briefly under the cold water, put some into each cup, and then poured the water in. "It wasn't supposed to boil, but I think it will still be okay." Placing the steaming cup in front of me, she turned, took something out of her silverware drawer, and put one in front of me and one next to her cup. "There. That's called a bombilla. You drink the tea out of that. But wait until it steeps for a few minutes." She returned to massaging my neck, and I was too weak to argue.

After a few minutes, she said, "Okay, it should be ready. Since you've never had it before, let me put some honey in. It will make it more palatable for you." Kasey brought the honey over from her cabinet and put in a teaspoon. "All right. Drink it slowly, it will still be hot."

"I know how to drink tea," I snapped, a little sharper than I had intended.

"You said you didn't drink tea."

"I don't. But I know how to drink hot beverages!"

"You need to chill, Lorry. Drink it."

"*You're* not drinking it. Are you trying to poison me?"

"Lorry, just drink it." Kasey picked up her own bombilla, placed it into her cup, and took a sip. "Oh, I love this stuff. Especially after a hard day. This will help you, Lorry. Please try it."

I took a sip out of the stupid straw. It tasted horrible. "I can't drink this."

"Let me get you more honey. This tea will help you, I promise." She put two more dripping teaspoons of honey into my cup. "Come on, drink it."

The honey made it easier to drink. Kasey resumed her massaging between sips of her own tea. I managed to drink the whole cup through the weird straw. And I don't know how long it was, and if it was the massaging or the tea, but suddenly, instead of feeling overwhelmed and trapped, I felt like I had everything under control. It was like clarity had blossomed in me, and I knew exactly what I must do. "Kasey, would you mind picking up Aiden for me? I'll call Pamela."

"Sure, Lorry. And you and Aiden will stay for dinner tonight."

I nodded. And I knew what kind of car I wanted. A RAV4. Light colored. Automatic remote start. Heated seats. And I knew exactly what I must do next. I had to find out who murdered Eddie.

CHAPTER TEN

KASEY'S KITCHEN HAD a pale yellow ceiling and
print wallpaper that Kasey and John let Lily pick out. It
had bright clowns on it. There were hardly any drawings
or markings in the entire kitchen—probably because she
was the one to pick it out.

I helped Kasey prepare dinner while Aiden and Lily
ran around the house like crazy people. Aiden never
acted that way at home, but at Kasey's I let him run free.
If I tried to rein him in while Lily ran wild, it wouldn't
be good for anybody. So I just let it happen. Lily was his
best friend in school—had been even before I became his
mommy—and I didn't want to hurt their dynamic. It
would just take a word from me to get Aiden to sit down
quietly and read, but I didn't want to do that. He got
enough reading at home anyway.

John Brannigan, Kasey's husband, came home right at
five o'clock, and gave me the obligatory hug and kiss on
the cheek. "I heard what happened to you today, Lorry.
I'm sorry you had to go through that." With his crewcut
and military bearing, he looked more like a football
player than a high school principal. It always struck me

as strange that a former marine and a principal would be so lenient with his own kids.

With my hands on my hips, I glared at Kasey and said, "See, Kasey? John didn't think I did it!"

She smiled. "Oh, he might have. He's more tactful than I am."

I rolled my eyes and looked at John. "I didn't do it, John. I couldn't stand the guy, but I didn't kill him."

His eyes twinkled. "Despite what Kasey said, I never thought you did it. I know you too well. There's no way you would risk losing Aiden for that creep."

I gave Kasey a playful shove that sent a handful of lettuce leaves falling to the floor. "See that, Kasey? John didn't think I did it!"

John called the kids into the kitchen. Aiden walked into the bathroom and washed his hands without my asking. He was such a good kid. John was right. I wouldn't do anything that would put me at risk of losing that boy.

Dinner consisted of a delicious meat loaf, mashed potatoes, and asparagus sauteed in real butter. John was kind enough not to mention any more about the murder, and I was certain that Kasey would tell him every nuance of the situation after I left.

Zandor sat in a high chair next to John's seat. In between his own food, John gave Zandor a spoonful of strained *stuff*. It was green. It didn't look particularly appetizing, but I wasn't six months old. Zandor seemed to like it. Some of the green stuff slid down his chin and onto the tray in front of him. With typical baby uncoordinated-ness, he somehow managed to pick it up. But instead of getting it into his own mouth, it landed on John, who scraped it off his shirt with Zandor's spoon and fed it to him again.

But the incident gave Lily an idea. A bad one. She picked up a handful of mashed potatoes and held them over her shoulder aimed at Aiden. He glanced at me, put both hands in his lap, and looked down. Lily plunked half of them back onto her plate and ate the other half out of her hand, licking her fingers when she was done. At least she didn't try to hit an unarmed man. Despite her unruly behavior, she was a good kid. You couldn't blame the kid if the parents didn't discipline her.

When dinner was over and after I had helped Kasey clean up the kitchen, John drove Aiden and me home. It was Rutledge—nothing was far away. So in five minutes we were in the safety of our own home. Aiden felt exhausted from the hard playing, so I dressed him in his blue feet pajamas with trains on them and put him in bed. Even as tired as he was, he still insisted on our nightly routine of reading to each other. It was his night to read to me, and that was the one concession he made. He allowed me to do the reading.

The book we were reading was *Alice's Adventures in Wonderland*, and we were on the eighth chapter. Aiden put his head on the pillow, and I could see him fighting to keep his eyes open. I read slowly and before I had finished the second page, Aiden's eyes had closed, and he was asleep. After kissing him on the forehead and tucking him in, I turned out the light, and retired to the living room.

It had been a hard day for me, too, but I wasn't ready to go to bed. I took a notebook and pen from the desk in the other room and then I sat down on the couch. Who could have murdered Eddie? Suspects. The first possibility would be Eddie killing himself. Since he had just had sex, maybe his girlfriend Rita Croft—if she was still his girlfriend—told him he was a lousy lover, and it bothered him so much he blew himself away. That one would be easy to check. I'd have to ask Billy if Eddie's fingerprints were on the gun. And he would have done it in my car just to punish me. For what, I didn't know. Oh, yes, I did. For not giving him money when he asked for it after we had separated. Being a degenerate gambler, Eddie always needed money for something.

So Eddie himself would be the first suspect. The second had to be his girlfriend—Rita Croft. Although I didn't know if she was still his girlfriend. If she was, then she would definitely be suspect number two.

Who else? Eddie had a lot of gambling debts. What were those guys' names who had come to the house a time or two? I felt myself flush with shame when I remembered the first time they came. They pushed their way into the house and had Eddie up against the wall when I scurried downstairs to see what was going on. One of them spotted me, ran up before I knew what was going on, and grabbed me from behind. Then—the thought of it still made me sick to my stomach—he put a gun to my head.

The other guy let Eddie go when he saw that the gun was on me. "Hey, Eddie. We're going to kill your little wifey if you don't come up with some money real quick like."

Eddie said, "All right! All right! I'll get the money!" Then he casually strolled into the kitchen, opened the back door, and shouted before he ran out, "Go ahead! Kill her! I'd rather keep the money!"

The guy who had been holding Eddie against the wall ran into the kitchen. When he came back, he shook his head. "He's gone."

The other guy let me go, put his gun back into his shoulder holster, and turned to me. "Lady, that guy is scum. If you were smart, you'd leave him and never come back." Then the two of them walked out the door. Good advice from a couple of hoodlums that I should have listened to. Next time they came back, a couple of years later, they couldn't believe I was still there. But they also didn't try to threaten Eddie with my well being. They already knew that wouldn't work.

And yes, I was that stupid. Even after he said he'd rather have his money than me *and* told them to kill me, I didn't leave. Not only that, but when he ran out the kitchen door, he didn't return home for a week, and when he did, he reeked of women's perfume. I ignored that, because I always did, and then asked him if he meant everything he said. He took me into his arms and said that he knew they wouldn't really kill me, and he had just said that so he could get away. And stupid me believed him. I really did have reason to kill him, didn't I?

CHAPTER ELEVEN

AFTER EATING BREAKFAST with Aiden and getting his lunch ready while he got dressed, I put a leash on Bingo, and then we stepped out of the house. And it was only then that I remembered we didn't have a car. Luckily, Bryan was right on the job, and he was standing there with one hand on the open door of his white Buick. "Hello, Lorry. Hello, Aiden."

Smiling, I said, "Hello, Bryan." Aiden looked up at me. "Aiden, this is Bryan. He's going to be helping Mommy for a while. And he's going to give us a ride to school today."

Aiden glanced at Bryan, said, "Hi, Bryan," and then stopped. "Mommy, I don't want a ride to school! I want to walk from the historical society like we always do!"

"All right, then. Bryan can drop us off there. Okay?"

"Yeah, okay."

The three of us climbed into the car. I buckled Aiden into the back, and Bingo jumped in beside him. Then I sat in the front with Bryan.

"This is a big car, Mommy. Bigger than ours."

"I know, Aiden. It's nice, isn't it?"

"Yeah. Can we get one like this?"

Before I could answer, Bryan spoke up. "Yes, Lorry, did you decide what kind of car you wanted?"

"Where's *our* car, Mommy?"

"Um, it's being looked at right now, Aiden." I wasn't going to lie to the kid, and that was as close as I could get to the truth without revealing the *real and awful truth* to him.

"Then can we get a car like this?"

Bryan looked at me. "I can arrange it. Just give me the word."

"No, this isn't my style."

Aiden jumped up and down in the seat—at least as much as he could with the seat belt holding him in. "Yes, Mommy! Yes! I like this car! Let's get one just like it!"

He was picking up bad habits from Lily—habits I didn't like at all. "Sorry, sweetie, but Mommy has decided that we're going to get a RAV4."

"Oh, Mommy! No! I want a—"

I turned around as much as I could with the seat belt holding *me* in. "No, Aiden. Now that's enough! I mean it!"

"Okay." He buried his head in Bingo's fur.

In precise detail, I explained to Bryan everything I wanted in a car. "You can buy it yourself. I don't need to be involved. And, um—" I pulled down the visor and slid the panel over so that I could use the vanity mirror to look at Aiden in the back. His head was still buried in Bingo's fur. "Um, after my car is *looked at*, will you take care of that, too?"

"Yes, no problem."

He pulled into the back of the historical society, and we got out of the car. "Goodbye, Bryan. Thank you for picking us up."

"Bye, Bryan," said Aiden. "Thanks for dropping us off here instead of the school. I like walking to school."

"I see that, Aiden. No problem. And you're welcome, Lorry. I should have your car for you today."

"That fast?"

"I'll see what I can do."

Aiden took my hand and pulled on it. "Come on, Mommy. I'll be late for school."

I closed the door of the car, and the three of us walked to school by our usual route. When we arrived, there was the same crowd, but they seemed to be paying a lot of attention to us. I thought it was my imagination, so I kissed Aiden goodbye and turned around to leave. Then I noticed there were a lot more kids around Aiden than usual. Maybe they were the kids who he was helping or something. It made me smile. My seven-year-old helping other kids learn how to read when six months ago, everyone thought that *he* couldn't learn to read. How ironic was that?

Bingo and I walked in the back door of the historical society and made our way to the front. The phone was ringing, but I thought I should open before I answered. It wasn't yet nine o'clock anyway. There was a crowd out there, bigger than I had ever seen before. That was unusual. Big groups almost always made arrangements in advance. Shrugging, I changed the sign to *Open* and unlocked the door. As soon as the door opened, the people piled in, pushing and shoving to get to the front. To get to *me*. They stuck their microphones in my face and snapped pictures of me. Bingo ran around in circles barking furiously, but they ignored him.

"Miss Lockharte, did you kill Eddie Keeley?"

"Ms." I corrected. "What?"

Someone held up a newspaper. The headlines were *Former Rutledge Heiress Accused of Killing Husband.* "He's my *ex*-husband!" Former heiress? I didn't realize that's what they called me. Would I be called an heiress again now once I got my mother's money? The reporters' voices filled the room, and the background noise was the incessant phone which never stopped ringing.

"So did you kill him?"

"No, I didn't kill him! What are you all doing here? Please leave!"

"We just want an interview, Miss Lockharte."

"Ms." I hated when people called me *miss*. It made me feel like an old maid. Ms. was more avant-garde and made me feel better. "Please get out." I tried pushing them back out the door, but there were too many of them. Not only that, but they kept snapping pictures of me with my arms out. What was I going to do?

Then I heard a voice at the front door, screaming from the back of the crowd. "Get out of here! All of you! Or I will call the sheriff! You are *trespassing*! Get out!" It was Petra. When they didn't move, she pulled her cell phone out of her purse and began tapping numbers. The reporters saw that, ambled out the door, and took their sweet time about it, too. When the last of them had left, Petra closed and locked the door behind them. After turning the sign on the door to *Closed*, she leaned over and hugged me. "Are you okay?"

"Thank you for saving me, Petra." She wore stacked heels, a too-short skirt, a ruffled blouse, and a raggedy sweatshirt on top—not a raggedy "like a rag" sweatshirt, but the kind that you pay good money for that already has holes in it. And still with her tattoos, piercings, and

54

pink hair. But we cannot choose our rescuers, right? Besides, Petra was a really great person, and as I've said before, I have the utmost respect for her. I don't sound like it, though, do I? I guess I'll have to work on that.

CHAPTER TWELVE

PETRA LEANED OVER me to answer the phone. I had been too frazzled to even think about it. "Rutledge Historical Society! . . . No! And don't call back!" She banged it into the cradle, but as soon as it was there, it rang again. "Rutledge Historical Society!" She didn't even say no the second time, just banged it back in its cradle. When it started ringing again immediately, she picked it up, pressed down on the receiver button and lay the phone on the desk beside the cradle. "Let's leave it off the hook for a while."

Petra Hamilton was the sixteen-year-old woman who worked with me at the Rutledge Historical Society. Prior to this summer, she only worked in the mornings and afternoons—before and after school. But starting in the summer, she began working full time. Now she wasn't on full time, but she still spent all day here so she could take the remainder of her high school classes online. And she was also taking college classes online. When she graduated, she would not only have her high school degree, but a two-year college degree as well. They only offered the program to exceptional students. Petra was exceptional.

She was also one of the weirdest people I had ever met. Not so much in actions, but in her looks. When I first met her, I used to call her the kaleidoscope girl—not to her face, of course. Back then she had pink and purple streaked hair and numerous piercings. Only the color of her hair had changed. Her hair was now a more subtle shade of pink. She had dispensed with the purple. But all her piercings—eyebrow, nose, tongue, *and* belly button—were still visible.

Today she wore a skirt that was way too short, even for high school, and a blouse that showed off her belly button ring. Didn't they have any dress code in school these days? Or did the kids who abused it hide out in safe places during times when they might be caught by the vice-principal? That's how we did it when I was in school, anyway.

At first I judged Petra harshly for the way she looked. When I got to know her, though, she was a responsible and reliable person who was generous and supportive of my initial troubles. Eddie troubles, that is. Eddie and I had just separated when I started the job, and he was giving me a lot of grief. Getting himself killed in my car so that I was the main suspect proved that he was still giving me grief even from the grave. Jerk. Anyway, I thought that Petra was awesome, and despite her freaky looks, she was solid. She had my respect. All of it.

"The etymology for paparazzi is interesting," Petra said. "Paparazzi, plural of paparazzo. It's from the name of Signor Paparazzo, a character in Federico Fellini's *La Dolce Vida*."

I shook my head. "Where do you get this stuff, Petra?"

She ignored me. "I'm going to call Martha about

staying closed for the day or until this is sorted out. And also about not answering the phone." She looked at me with her eyebrows raised. "I'm assuming you didn't do it, right?"

Leave it to Petra to say it like it is. That was okay with me. I was a "calls 'em like I sees 'em kind of girl" myself. I also knew Petra well enough to know that if I said I did it, she would just go from there, helping me where she could. "Right. I didn't do it, but whoever killed him, did it in my car! My wonderful Taurus that was just like the Taurus that Eddie wrecked! But it doesn't matter now—at least car-wise—because I'm getting a new one."

"Another Taurus? You should reconsider that. You're having bad luck with Tauruses."

"That's what I've finally figured out. I'm getting a RAV4. Bryan's picking it up for me today."

"Who's Bryan? A new beau?"

"New beau? That implies there was an old beau. No, and no. My mother's attorneys sent him. He got here so quickly, I thought maybe you called and told them I needed help. But apparently they've been following me and videoing me! That's how they knew I was filing for divorce and trying to adopt Aiden."

Petra nodded her head. "Yeah, we were wondering how they did that. Now we know."

"Yeah. Now we know."

Petra disappeared into her office and then returned. "Hey, this came for you yesterday." She handed me a messenger envelope from my mother's attorneys.

"Oh, yeah. Bryan told me this was coming."

"Listen, I'm going to call Martha now."

"Thanks, Petra."

Sticking the envelope into the middle top drawer of

the desk—I didn't want to deal with it right then—I looked out the window and there were still reporters hanging around, snapping pictures of me. They had probably been doing that while I was talking to Petra. It was a business, so there weren't even any blinds to close. There was no way I was going to sit there all day and allow them free access to my pretty face. I turned my chair toward the fish tank to give the reporters a good view of my broad back and tried to relax by watching the smooth movements of the fish.

It might have been five minutes, it might have been twenty, but I finally felt more relaxed. Then I heard a sharp tapping on the door. I turned around and there stood Sheriff Billy, tapping on the glass door with his gun.

Frowning, I stood up and opened the door for him. "Have you come to arrest me *again*?" Bingo stood at the ready, but didn't growl at him like the day before.

Billy walked in and closed the door behind him. "I didn't arrest you yesterday; I *detained* you. There's a difference."

"You threw me into that concrete cell. You locked the door."

"Oh, Lorry, I hardly threw you in. Come on. What was I supposed to do? I found you with your ex-husband's dead body."

"You could have believed me, Billy—I thought we were friends." He looked down, and I sat down and turned my chair toward the computer, so all he could see was my back. I wanted him to leave and leave me alone.

Billy turned my chair around and kneeled down so we were face to face. Bingo stood there keeping watch to make sure he didn't try anything. "Lorry, I came over to apologize. I'm sorry. I'm sorry that I didn't trust you. I should have, and I know that now."

I leaned forward so our noses were almost touching. "So now that the DNA test came back to prove me innocent, you can say that. Some friend you are!" Crossing my arms over my chest, I leaned back again.

"Lorry, the DNA test doesn't come back that fast. I just acted without thinking. It was just a reflex action— you know, from my training: I find someone with a dead body, then I have to bring them in. I'm sorry. I made a mistake. Haven't you ever made a mistake?"

"Yeah. I married Eddie."

"Lorry," Petra called from the other room, "that's the wrong thing to say if you're trying to prove yourself innocent of killing the dude!"

Billy stood up to his full six-foot-four-inch height and looked down at me. "She's right, Lorry. You can't disparage the guy you're accused of killing."

"I didn't think you were accusing me anymore."

He looked out the window at the reporters who had withdrawn across the street. "I'm not. But *they* still are."

CHAPTER THIRTEEN

THE REASON THE reporters had retreated across the street was because Billy had threatened to arrest them. That's why his gun was out when he tapped on the door. He had to get rough with them—as rough as Billy would get. He was a tough guy, but I would describe him as tough *and* tender. And when I thought about it, he chased those reporters away *for me*.

"Thank you for doing that, Billy. I appreciate it."

"It was the least I could do. And I also wanted to make this all up to you by taking you out to dinner—"

"Absolutely not. I wouldn't even—"

"Um, after I solve the case."

"You still don't believe me—at least, not all the way. Do you?" Not waiting for an answer, I stalked off to the back room, with Bingo at my heels.

From the back, I heard Billy say to Petra, "I think you can open again now. Those reporters will stay away. If they don't, just call me. Or you can threaten them by saying you'll call me. That will probably work." I heard his heavy sigh even from the back room. "I guess I'll go now. That apology didn't go over very well."

Petra whispered something to him that I couldn't hear, and then I heard Billy go out the door. Rushing up, I stopped at Petra's desk. "And just *what* did you whisper to him?"

She laughed. "I told him that he should have asked you out months ago."

"And what did that big bully say?" He wasn't a big bully, but I wasn't going to call him a jerk, because I reserved that for Eddie, dead or alive.

"He said, 'Too late for that now.'" Petra looked at me with a sad expression on her face. "Sorry, Lorry."

"That's okay, Petra. It is what it is."

"Billy said we could probably open again, but if you don't want to, it's okay. Martha said that was fine."

"Naw. Let's go ahead and open. I think Billy put the scare to those reporters so they won't return—at least not for a while." I marched to the front door, unlocked it, and changed the sign to *Open*. Then I sat down at my desk and turned on the computer to check my email.

The computer was still booting up when I heard the jingle of the front door opening. Turning to see who it was, I saw my nemesis, Renee Croft. She was also the sister of Eddie's girlfriend, Rita Croft. What could she possibly want with me, I wondered.

Renee, usually one of the best dressed in high school, wore an expensive pant suit that looked like it didn't fit her right—definitely unusual for someone who had most of her clothes tailor-made. And she hadn't gained or lost weight—that I could tell, anyway.

She closed the door behind her and with her eyes narrowed at me, she held out the morning paper and tapped it hard with her other hand. "You!" she shouted. "*You* killed Eddie because he was with my *sister*! I always knew you were a jealous *shrew*, but I didn't think you'd go this far!"

I hated that she was above me shouting down at me like that, so I stood up. Although she was still taller than me, I felt better standing. "Renee, I didn't kill Eddie. I don't care what that paper says. I didn't do it." Not raising my voice, I tried to remain calm, hoping that it would calm her down as well. I had read that sometimes works. This was a case where it didn't.

"You did it! I *know* you did it! It has your name all over it! Killed him in your car, did you? What a *stupid* witch you are!"

"Did you ever consider," I said quietly, "that maybe your sister and Eddie got into a fight, and *she* killed him? I know from experience that Eddie can get on someone's nerves."

"Rita is in San Francisco with our *aunt*! She's been gone for a week! So she couldn't possibly have done it! Why don't you admit your dirty little crime and make it simpler for everybody?" She was still screaming.

From the corner of my eye, I saw that Petra had come silently out of her office and was standing watching the fireworks. She didn't say a thing; she just watched wide-eyed.

"I can't admit it, Renee, because I didn't do it. Now why don't you go home and chill?"

"Not until I've done this—"

Renee stepped forward with her arm drawn back and was getting ready to swing it forward to slap me across the face when Bingo barked once as a warning. She glared at him, but the one bark didn't seem to scare her. She drew her hand back again, this time balling her hand into a fist. And Bingo came unglued, barking and jumping at her feet, but not biting. I'll have to teach him better than that. Sometimes a good bite is exactly what is needed.

Renee dropped her fist, but she swung her leg back so she could kick at Bingo. Petra stepped forward and said, "If you kick that dog, you'll be sorry. I'll bite you myself, and it won't be pretty!" Good ole Petra bared her teeth and growled at Renee. Bingo followed suit. Renee put her foot back under her and opened the door. Glaring at me, she said, "I'll get you for this yet!"

CHAPTER FOURTEEN

"THANKS FOR RESCUING me, Petra. Again."

"Naw. I didn't rescue you that time, Lorry. I rescued *him*." She knelt down and scooped Bingo up in her arms while he covered her face with wet doggie kisses.

A minute later, Rocky the cat—so named because of an encounter with a raccoon in his youth—strolled in, causing me to sneeze, and my eyes to itch. I was allergic to cats, but working on it. Petra put Bingo down, and Rocky rubbed up against him, meowing. Bingo smelled the cat's butt and wagged his tail. They were best friends.

It didn't start out that way, though. When Eddie and I were still married, through a series of deft manipulations, Eddie had made me give Bingo away. I used to visit him until the family moved to Phoenix. And then I thought I'd never see him again. But shortly after starting my job at Rutledge Historical Society, the family planned to move back east and couldn't take Bingo with them, so they found me, thankfully, and gave him back, much to my delight.

When I first brought Bingo into work, he and Rocky had a standoff. With a hunched back and a twitching tail, Rocky stood there hissing his displeasure. Bingo gave one sharp bark and was ready to spring when I told him to sit and stay. After being so long away from me, I wasn't sure if he would still remember his training, but he did. He sat there and looked at the cat. Rocky, still hunched and hissing, looked back. Bingo waited a few minutes and then laid down. It didn't take long for Rocky to stop hissing and relax. Rocky sat down. The two stared at each other without moving. Bingo stood up and Rocky crouched. Instead of asking Bingo to sit back down, I waited to see what would happen. Bingo tired of standing and sat again. Rocky relaxed. They stared at each other. Finally, Rocky stood up and walked as if on tiptoes over to Bingo. They sniffed noses. When Bingo started to stand, Rocky backed off. Eventually, they developed an uneasy *acquaintance*. But it didn't take long for them to become pals, and now, just a few short months later, they loved each other.

Rocky meowed up at me, and I patted my lap. He jumped up and rubbed his face against mine, which made me sneeze. Petra had told me when I first started work here that it was possible to rise above allergies and not let them affect you. And my allergy to Rocky was *better*, but still not gone. I sneezed again. Although I used to hate cats, this one—I petted Rocky's sleek fur—I owed my life to. I rubbed my chin on the top of his head and put him down. Bingo jumped up in my lap. He wasn't exactly jealous, but he wanted Rocky to know that my lap was *his* property. He was willing to share it, but not give it over completely. I hugged Bingo and put him back on the floor.

"So what are you going to do about *her*?" asked Petra.

"And them." I motioned across the street to the

reporters still hanging out there. Their telephoto lenses probably captured me kissing Rocky and Bingo. I hoped they got my good side. "The only thing I can do. Find the real killer. That's the only way they'll leave me alone."

"Where are you going to start?"

"Well, first I have to make sure that Eddie didn't kill himself in my car. That would be just like him—ruining a perfectly good car and not to mention my reputation. And then I have to find out if Renee was telling the truth about her sister. You know, if she was really in San Francisco."

"How are you going to find out?"

Shrugging, I said, "I guess I have to call Billy, but I doubt if he'll tell me anything."

"He might surprise you—he feels bad about yesterday."

I put the phone back on the hook, and it immediately rang again. "Rutledge Historical Society." When I realized it was a reporter, I smacked the phone down in the cradle. It rang again. Picking it up but without answering, I pressed the receiver button and lay it on the desk where Petra had left it. Then I rummaged through my purse to find my cell phone. Pulling it out, I tapped the number. "May I please speak to Sheriff Billy? It's Lorry Lockharte calling."

The dispatcher put me on hold, and while I waited I chatted with Petra. "If Eddie didn't kill himself, and his girlfriend Rita didn't do it, I'm not sure where else to look. I've been out of his life for months now. Who knows what kind of predicament he could have gotten himself into?"

"His girlfriend Rita might know."

"Yeah, like she would tell me anything after her sister comes over here accusing me of Eddie's murder. Rita was never the brightest bulb, so she'll just believe Renee."

Our conversation was interrupted when Billy suddenly came on the phone. "Hello, Billy. I was wondering if I could ask you a couple of questions about Eddie's murder. . . . All right, goodbye."

"He said *no*? I can't believe he told you no."

"Actually he said he'd be right over."

CHAPTER FIFTEEN

PETRA RETURNED TO her desk to study, and I waited expectantly for Billy's patrol car to pull up out front. So when I heard the rear door open and footsteps coming from the back room, it surprised me.

"Hi, again, Billy," said Petra.

"Hey, Petra." I heard him give her a quick kiss on the head. They were close—Billy always kissed her on the head. He was paying the costs for Petra to take the college classes online, much to her father's dismay. Her father was a perennial drunk, and Petra was lucky that he had agreed to the arrangement.

Billy stepped into the room. "Hello, Lorry."

He said it with no enthusiasm, and it made me wonder why he had been so willing to come over to talk. Had he come over to arrest me after finding new evidence that implicated me? Speak up and get it over with, I thought.

"Hi, Billy. I was wondering if Eddie's fingerprints were on the gun—that maybe he killed himself in my car. That would be something he would do, because he knew how much I loved that Taurus."

"There were no fingerprints on the gun. They had been wiped off. And Eddie wasn't killed in your car."

"He wasn't? How can you be sure?"

"I'm a cop. I know these things." When I glared at him, he continued. "Besides the incidental blood from his wounds, there was no blood, no evidence of, um, bodily *debris*."

Puzzled, I tilted my head and looked at him for a minute. Then it occurred to me what he meant. "Oh! You mean there were none of Eddie's *brains* inside my car!"

Billy coughed to stifle a laugh. "Um, yes, that's what I mean. So whoever killed him moved him into your car. And there was his rain-splattered shirt that you pointed out. He was moved while it was still raining. My thought is that he was either killed in someone else's car or killed elsewhere and then *put* into another car and moved to yours. Which means somewhere, there's another car with at least some incidental blood in it. Would you have any idea who might have motive to kill Eddie—you know, besides you?"

I stood up, put my hands on my hips, and narrowed my eyes at him. "You dare say that to me now? *After* apologizing?" It was then I noticed the slight smile at the corner of his mouth. Billy was a funny guy. It was one of the reasons I liked him.

"Jeez, Lorry, I was joking." He frowned. "Guess it isn't the right time for that, is it?"

"Considering those vultures are still out there probably with an ultra-sensitive microphone pointed at the building, I'd say, no, it isn't the right time. It will *never* be the right time." I sat back down, and Bingo jumped into my lap.

Billy bent over to pet Bingo and then thought better of it and pulled back his hand. "All right, sorry. Do you know anyone else with a motive?"

"Eddie and I haven't been together in months. What about his girlfriend, Rita Croft? She was supposedly in San Francisco with her aunt. Can you find out if that's true? Isn't it usually the spouse or girlfriend or whatever?"

"You're still the spouse, Lorry."

"We're getting a divorce. It's almost final. Oh, wait. I guess I don't need one now."

"No, you don't. And yes, I can follow up on the girlfriend. Can you think of anyone else? I know Eddie was a gambler. How about outstanding gambling debts? Could anyone be after him for that?"

"Oh! Yeah! There were those two thugs who came to our house a couple of times!"

"Do you know their names?"

"I don't have a clue. They were big and burly and mean, and they had a gun." I didn't mention that they held said gun to my head. He didn't need to know how stupid I had been to stay with Eddie through that and all the other degradations he put me through. It would be even more of a motive for murder. "I'm sure he knew them from Coyote Moon." I meant the casino, not the city of Coyote Moon.

"What do they look like besides big and burly? Could you sit down with an artist and describe them?"

"No, I doubt it. It was years ago, and it was under rather precarious circumstances. But I know that I'd recognize them again if I saw them."

Then we heard the back door open and close, and small footsteps come running from the back area. We

71

both turned to see who it was, but I already knew. It was Aiden. And when he got close enough, I saw that his face was red-streaked from crying and tears were still flowing down his face. Dressed in blue jeans and an *I love Batman* t-shirt that was only half-tucked in, he looked pathetic, poor kid. He ran straight into my arms.

"Mommy! Mommy! They're calling me a son of a murderer! You're not a murderer, are you?" Then he gave Billy a furtive glance. "*He* won't put you in jail again, will he?" Aiden buried his face in my neck.

CHAPTER SIXTEEN

THE PROBLEM WAS, Billy and Aiden were close. Billy hadn't just come to his birthday party, he had also taken him several places—without me—including fishing and to a car race in Coyote Moon. I thought it would be good for Aiden to have a male influence in his life, and Billy enjoyed it. So for Aiden to react like that to Billy must have given Billy quite a shock. First Bingo growling at him and now this.

"No, honey, I won't put your mommy in jail. Yesterday was a mistake. I'm sorry." Billy reached out to Aiden, but Aiden stayed buried in my arms and wouldn't look at him. "Your mommy's not going to jail anymore."

Aiden turned his head toward Billy, tears still streaming down. "But everyone thinks she's a murderer, and there are no other suspects."

"He really gets right to the matter at hand, doesn't he?" Billy knelt down so he could look at Aiden at eye level. "We'll find the real murderer, and your mommy will *not* be going to jail."

"Do you promise?"

I saw Billy's eyes briefly raise to the ceiling, and I knew

why. If there were no other suspects, and I was the *only* suspect, then maybe I *would* be going to jail. People had been convicted from less evidence than they had on me.

Billy nodded his head. "Yes. I promise."

Aiden must have believed him because he leaned back from me and put his arms out for Billy to hold him. Billy sighed and wrapped his arms around Aiden.

Aiden's tears started anew. "I felt so scared. I thought Mommy was going to jail. And everybody was making fun of me." He glanced at me briefly. "Everybody except Lily. She's still my friend." Burying his head in Billy's neck, he continued. "I don't want to go back to school anymore, Mommy. I don't want to go."

When Bingo saw Aiden in Billy's arms, it must have convinced him, too, because he rubbed himself on Billy's feet and gave a sharp little bark, like "Me, too!" That broke the tension in the room and made Aiden laugh.

Billy put Aiden down on the floor and put his hands on his shoulders. Then he looked at me as if asking permission—to do what, I didn't know—but I nodded. "Listen, big guy. Those kids making fun of you is called bullying. And we don't allow bullying in our schools here in Rutledge. I'll go to that school and make sure they know that. Would that make you feel better?"

"A little. Would you arrest them if they did it again?"

"No. Nobody is being arrested. But I'll talk to Mrs. Reilly to see if we can get them suspended from school. Is that okay with you?"

"I don't want anybody to get in trouble." That was my boy Aiden—always concerned for the other guy. We'd have to have a talk about that. Not standing up for himself could be part of the problem.

"Listen, Aiden. What they're saying to you is not

acceptable. Someone needs to tell on them. Are you strong enough to do that?" The tears dripped out of Aiden's eyes, but he nodded. "Good," said Billy. "I thought you were. This is what I want you to do. First, do you have any friends besides Lily?"

"Well, some of the kids in my old reading group might be my friends."

"All right. Then whenever you go outside to recess or lunch, make sure you're with a friend. When the bullies say something to you, maintain eye contact. Do you know what that means?" Aiden nodded, and Billy continued. "If they yell at you, don't yell back. Stay calm. And use their name when speaking to them."

"Do I have to hit them?"

Billy shook his head. "No. I don't want you to hit them. Have they hit you?"

"No, they're just calling me and Mommy names."

"All right. Do what I say, and you should be fine. I'll call Mrs. Reilly about having an assembly where I can give a talk on bullying. And you don't have to go to school the rest of today or tomorrow. I'll tell her you won't be there. Is that all okay with you?" Aiden nodded, and Billy pulled him into another hug. "That's my boy. You'll be fine."

"Thank you, Sheriff Billy."

Billy stood up to his full height and looked at Aiden. "You're welcome. And don't worry. Everything will work out."

Aiden stepped over to me, grabbed my arm, and laid his head on it. "I hope so."

"I'm leaving now. Lorry, take care of yourself. And I'm going tonight to Coyote Moon to see if I can find those guys."

"You're not going dressed like *that*, are you?" He wore his Smokey Bear hat, dark brown pants and a light brown shirt. And don't forget the shiny star on his chest —just like Marshall Dillon.

He smirked. "How *should* I go dressed? Wear a dress and heels?" When I closed my eyes and shook my head, he continued. "No, I'll be in my civvies. Not to worry." And he walked out of the room toward the back, the way he had come in.

I looked down at my dress. It was a black and white check with three-quarter sleeves. And I had shoes to match. And it wouldn't be tonight, because Billy was going tonight. But tomorrow night, if Billy hadn't found them yet, I would go to the casino to look for the two bums that had held a gun to my head and who might've killed Eddie.

CHAPTER SEVENTEEN

THE REST OF the afternoon passed without incident, except one. Martha had sent over some typing for me to do, and I was busy with that, while Aiden sat at Petra's desk, working on his coloring book that we kept there. A man, a woman, and a young boy knocked at the door and pointed toward the back. I shrugged and opened the door.

"We know you're closed, but we're leaving town first thing in the morning and we wanted to see the clothing exhibit. My son"—she pushed the boy in front of her —"doesn't believe boys used to wear dresses."

"Yeah, sure, come on inside." I didn't know what harm it could do. They wore jeans and hiking boots and looked like they had just returned from a hike. They seemed like legitimate guests, not reporters.

The woman and son came in, followed by the man. As they walked past me, the boy turned around and pointed his finger at me. "Aren't you that woman who killed her husband?"

Aiden pushed his way into the room and looked up at the kid who was several years older and several inches taller. "What's your name?" asked Aiden in a commanding voice. At least it was commanding for a seven-year-old. I had no idea what he was doing.

"What?" said the boy, as his parents tried to push him toward the back.

"I said"—Aiden raised his voice—"what's your name?"

"Kendyn," said the boy.

Aiden poked a finger at the boy's chest, without touching him. "Kendyn, my mommy didn't kill anybody, and I don't want to hear you say that again!" Bingo stood beside Aiden and barked once softly at the stranger.

The boy looked down at Aiden, raised his hands over his head as if he was surrendering, and said, "Yeah, all right, all right." Then he turned and walked toward the back with his parents.

In the other room, Petra chuckled as Aiden came and buried his head on my shoulder. "I protected you, Mommy. I stood up for you like Sheriff Billy said."

"That was very good, Aiden. Thank you."

"And I wasn't scared, either." He sniffled, and I noticed tears slowly working their way down his face.

When the family left, I locked the door, and if I heard a knock, I'd stand up and walk to the back without looking at who it was. Aiden stayed with me the rest of the afternoon and colored on the floor beside Bingo. By the end of the afternoon, I wondered where Bryan was with my new car.

"Hey, guys, can I have a ride home?" asked Petra.

"Bryan should have been back here with my car already. I don't know where he is."

"Maybe he's in the back. I'll go check!" Aiden ran off

before I had a chance to say anything. From the back I heard the door open and close, and Aiden call out, "He's out there. And our new car is exactly like his!" I could hear Aiden jumping up and down before he ran back to the front.

I stood up and grabbed my purse. Before Eddie died, I used to have to lock it up in my drawer, because there was no telling when he might pop in and take either the purse or the money inside or both. But now that he was dead, I didn't have to do that anymore. Having him dead was providing me more and more advantages, but I'd keep all that to myself—at least until his killer was caught.

"Come on, Petra. We'll take you home. I don't think it's our car, though. It's probably still Bryan's."

Aiden jumped up and down. "No, it's ours! It's ours!" He put his coloring book and crayons away and ran to the back again ahead of us.

Petra and Bingo and I walked out the back door and locked it. Bryan, always the impeccable dresser with a black suit, white dress shirt, and royal blue tie, was standing leaning against his white Buick with Aiden holding onto his fingers and jumping up and down in front of him. He seemed so different from when I first met him and thought he was uptight and aggressive. I supposed he could still be that way, but with me, he had only been kind and accommodating. Of course that might be in his job description from my mother's attorneys, but still, kind was kind, and that was always good.

"Sorry I couldn't get your car today, Lorry. I'm picking it up in Phoenix tomorrow. Hope that's okay."

"Yeah, it's fine. No hurry—as long as I have you as my

chauffeur!" Tomorrow night, I'd have the car and I could drive to Coyote Moon to look for the two thugs. "We're going to take Petra home tonight, all right?"

"Sure thing. Hop in."

Petra didn't even have to tell Bryan where she lived. He drove right up to the shabby house with the even shabbier lawn and dropped her off. "Thanks for the ride!" Petra said as she got out of the car. "Bye!"

When Bryan turned onto our street, cars lined it from one end to the other, with people trampling all over our front lawn. "I guess it was too much to hope that they wouldn't find out where you lived," said Bryan as he double parked in front of my house. Two cars were parked in the driveway, and it was no one that I knew. "Come on, I'll walk you inside." He opened his door.

Just then we heard a siren, and Billy's patrol car came squealing around the corner and pulled up behind Bryan. "I guess Billy boy is going to help you out here."

"He's not *Billy boy*," said Aiden. "He's *Sheriff* Billy!"

"Ah. My mistake," said Bryan, closing his door.

Billy, with his flashers still flashing, pulled out a megaphone and announced, "All cars not belonging to people living on this block will cease and desist. Go back where you came from. I am closing this street to all outside traffic. If you do not have legitimate business here, you will be arrested for trespassing. Now please leave."

When the people got into their cars and started their engines, Billy walked over to Bryan's car and opened the door for me and Aiden. "Hello, Bryan," he said without looking at him. "Come on, Lorry, Aiden, I'll walk you inside." Bingo jumped out of the car first, and we followed.

Most of the cars had left, but there were still a few lingerers snapping pictures. Billy pointed a finger at them, scowled, and escorted us all the way to the house. I opened the door and ushered Aiden inside. "Thank you, Billy. I appreciate it."

"It's the least I can do, Lorry." Then he turned around and moved toward the cars that were still hanging around.

I didn't wait to see what would happen. Closing the door, I leaned with my back up against it. We were finally home. And safe.

CHAPTER EIGHTEEN

AFTER SUCH AN intense day, I didn't feel much like cooking. While I changed clothes, I tried to figure out if I had any leftovers that were meal-worthy. Then the doorbell rang. Bingo barked. Aiden called out from his room, "Who would that be?" And I walked to the door wondering the same thing.

When I looked through the small glass window onto the front porch, I saw a pizza delivery man. I'd seen enough television movies to know a red flag when I saw one. There was no way I was going to open the door when I hadn't ordered pizza.

The guy holding the pizza knocked again and said in a loud voice, "Pizza delivery!"

From the safety of a closed door, I said, "I didn't order any pizza."

"This is from Sheriff Billy. He said to tell you that if you wouldn't have dinner with him, then he'd bring dinner to you."

"Is Billy coming over too, then?" I asked through the still closed door.

"No. He said he has to drive over to Coyote Moon

tonight."

I opened the door and inhaled the fresh, rich scent of a pepperoni pizza. The guy knew too many details to be fake. He handed me the pizza. It was extra large, and it was still hot. "Wait and I'll get you a tip."

"No need, Ma'am. Sheriff Billy gave me that, too. He said he owed you."

Again that was Billy. "Well, thank you very much. And thank Billy for me, too."

"Oh, I won't be seeing him tonight, Ma'am. Goodbye! Enjoy the pizza!"

The guy walked out to the truck with a plastic pizza displayed on the top. On the door was a picture of a delectable pizza and their phone number.

Aiden had finished whatever he was doing in his room and ran into the living room without his shoes on. "Pizza! Pizza! We're having pizza for dinner! Yay!" He ran into the kitchen in front of me with Bingo on his heels. Then he set the table. Aiden was a good kid, and I appreciated him every minute.

"Thank you, Your Highness. You get the first slice. Do you have a preference, M'lord?" I opened the box and held it out for him to see. He pointed to the biggest piece in the box, and I scooped it out with a purple pizza knife that I got from the Dollar Store and flopped it onto his plate. "Your wish is my command."

He giggled and dug in. I picked out a smaller piece for myself and followed his example. We both sat there oooing and aaahing and praising Sheriff Billy's generosity. After dinner, Aiden sat down to read while I cleaned the kitchen, which consisted of rinsing off the plates, putting them into the dishwasher, and sticking the leftover pizza, box and all, into the refrigerator.

When I finished, I walked into the living room where Aiden was. "Hey, kiddo. You want to watch a short video? A cartoon or something?" That didn't seem to impress Aiden, so I upped the stakes. "How about a science Ted Talk?" That made him lift his head, but then he shook it from side to side.

"Naw, thanks, I'm in a good part in my book." He was reading the eighth book in the Harry Potter series. I had wanted to use those books to read aloud during our bedtime reading sessions, but Aiden was too impatient, and wanted to read them by himself so he wouldn't have to wait so long to find out what happened.

Sitting beside him, I grabbed the time-travel romance book I was reading and opened it. We sat there like that for an hour, and then I got him ready for bed. "Whose turn is it to read about Alice?" I knew it was his turn since I had read the night before, but if he wanted to get out of it, I wanted to let him.

"It's my turn. Do you mind if I read some of last night's? I think I fell asleep while you were reading."

I smiled at him. "Sure thing, kiddo." Aiden did not like to miss a word of any book he was reading. I was the same way. Showing him the place, I leaned back in the chair beside his bed and listened to him read.

When he finished the chapter, he put the bookmark in the book and handed it to me. "That's all for tonight. I'm tired. You probably are, too."

"You're right there, kiddo. I am tired."

"Sheriff Billy said I didn't have to go to school tomorrow. Are you still going to make me?"

I shook my head. "No. Billy said you didn't have to go. If I had a problem with that, then I would have already said so. You don't have to go. You'll come to the office with me. Bring your book. I think you'll get bored coloring for all those hours."

I kissed him good night, tucked him in, and Bingo jumped on the bed. Aiden kissed us both good night, and I turned out the light and retired to the living room.

Reading for a while longer, I finally put the book down. After letting Bingo out for his last nighttime outing, I crawled into bed, turned out my light, and fell asleep. Sometime in the middle of the night, Bingo woke me up walking around on my bed and growling. But since I heard nothing, I thought he was imagining it. He wasn't.

CHAPTER NINETEEN

THE FOLLOWING MORNING began with a shout and a cry. Aiden came flying through my door and made a flying leap onto my bed, just missing me. Then he snuggled up beside me.

"I love you so much, Mommy! And I'm so glad you're not a murderer and not going to jail!"

Bingo wanted to get in on the fun, too, so he jumped on my stomach and pressed his cold, wet nose first on me and then on Aiden. We both pushed him away, but he burrowed back in, not wanting to miss anything.

This was so unlike Aiden who normally read quietly in his bed until I came in to "wake" him. The present awful situation had us acting outside of ourselves. The three of us enjoyed the warmth of the cuddling until I had to spoil everything and get up to make breakfast.

"Aww, Mom. Just a little longer," said Aiden. Bingo whined in agreement.

"Time for breakfast, gang!" I pulled out from Aiden's grasp, stepped out of bed, stretched and put on my pink, fluffy slippers. "You, young man, go read while I get organized. I'll be in to get you soon."

Aiden slid off the bed, gave me a quick hug, and ran from the room, with Bingo following close behind. I watched them go and thought again how grateful I was to have Aiden *and* Bingo in my life. Then I called Bingo so he could go outside for his morning constitutional.

A half hour later I knocked on Aiden's door for him to come to breakfast. "Eggs, oatmeal, or cereal today?"

"Pancakes!"

"It's a school day. Eggs or oatmeal?" We only had pancakes on the weekend. He loved the real maple syrup, but it revved him up. So I wasn't going to feed him that on a school day—whether or not he'd be at school.

"Cereal!"

Aiden sat at the table, and I poured the milk into the bowl for him. Then I put two glasses of orange juice on the table, one for him and one for me. The bell rang for my soft-boiled egg, so I turned off the burner, pulled it from the water with a spoon, and ran it under cold water. When it felt cooler to the touch, I put it in the egg holder with the little tray on the bottom for the egg shells.

"Aiden, don't forget to bring your book with you today. Maybe two if you're close to finishing."

"I only have the one, and I *am* almost finished. Can we go to the library today?"

"I'll see how it goes at work. Take one of mine, just in case."

He grinned at me. "I'll take my chances on the library." Aiden was very clear about the books he wanted to read—and he didn't want to read any of mine. Except for the classics that we read at night, he always liked to pick out his own books.

"Suit yourself!"

I cleared the table, put the dishes into the dishwasher

—my little egg holder on the top shelf—and then made Aiden's lunch, while he got dressed. When I got dressed, I considered my outfit carefully, because I still planned to go to the casino, and I probably wouldn't have time to change. Probably, just a regular work outfit would suffice, with low heels. So I put on my blue skirt, with the matching blue and yellow frilly blouse. Then I decided on my three-inch heels instead, because I thought the extra elevation made me look slimmer. Not slim, mind you, *slimmer.*

I snapped the leash on Bingo's collar, made sure that Aiden had his lunch and his book, and we stepped out the door. Bryan was just pulling up in front of the house, and the three of us walked toward him. He jumped out of the car looking concerned.

"Lorry!" he called out. "Don't turn around!"

Rebel that I am, always was, and always will be said, "Why not?" and turned around. Which of course made Aiden turn around. I clapped a hand over my mouth, and Aiden screamed and threw his arms around me. Bingo barked at the excitement in Aiden's voice. Behind us, in a blood-like dripping red, someone had painted the word *murderer* on our white front door.

I looked around to see some of the neighbors outside pointing toward our door. Not one of them greeted us. Not one of them said they were sorry about the vandalism. How could they if they believed it was true? I was the one found with the body and the one who had the biggest motive. Not only that, but I was the *only* suspect. Next thing, they'd be running me out of town on a rail. Oh wait, there was no rail. Well, a bus would do in a pinch.

Bryan, on his cell phone, came running out to us and

ushered the three of us into the car. A second later, I heard a siren and knew who Bryan had called. Billy bounded out of his patrol car practically while it was still moving. He looked at the door, shook his head with a frown, and strode over to Bryan's car.

"Are you both all right?"

"Just a little shaky, that's all." Although Aiden had his head buried in my arm and was softly crying.

Billy glanced back at the house and shook his head. "I have a feeling about this, and I don't think it's just vandalism. I think the murderer himself did this. If he can get the public to think you are the only suspect, it would only protect him."

I looked at Billy and shook my head. Although I didn't want to say anything, I believed that Billy was wrong. This wasn't done by the murderer. This was done by my nemesis, Renee Croft.

CHAPTER TWENTY

I WANTED TO leave the scene of the crime—er, vandalism—thinking that as long as we stayed in front of our defiled house, Aiden probably wouldn't calm down. And Billy leaning in the window of Bryan's car didn't help.

"You're not going to arrest my mommy, are you?"

"Aiden, I've already told you that I'm not going to arrest your mommy," Billy said a touch too harshly.

My interpretation of that was he thought maybe he *would* have to arrest me. If I was the only suspect, the town would start pressing him for action. And I had a lot going for me—you know, as a suspect. The fact that I didn't do it mattered a lot less than the expediency of solving the crime. If Billy weren't my friend, I would probably already be in county instead of just an hour in the Rutledge holding cell. But how long could he hold out if there were no other suspects?

"Lorry, I need to see you later today. Will you be in all day?" His voice still had an edge to it.

"Yes, all day."

Aiden tugged on my arm. "What about the library,

Mommy?"

"Oh, yeah. We're going to the library. So I'll be gone for a while."

"All right, I'll call first."

"Okay. Bye, Billy." I wanted to get out of there, and he was delaying us. Aiden would be late for school if we didn't hurry. Oh, wait. Aiden wasn't going to school. Still, I pressed the button to roll the window up. Billy stood there with his hand on the window blocking it.

"Hey, Lorry. You look really nice today." He took his hand off the window and stepped back.

"Thanks. Bye, Billy." I finished rolling the window up, and as Bryan drove away, I looked in the side mirror and saw Billy watching the car pull away.

It wasn't until we reached the end of the street that I saw all the cars lined up on both sides of the street. "Oh, no. Not them again."

"They're probably not going to go away until you deal with them."

"Then I guess they're not going away."

"Lorry, Billy boy there likes you."

"Bryan! It's *Sheriff* Billy!" said Aiden.

"You know, that's what Petra says. And you know what? If he does, he sure hasn't shown it to me. I've been waiting for him to ask me out for months."

"Well, there's no way he could do that now with the murder hanging over him like this. And you the main suspect."

"If I'm the main suspect, why doesn't he arrest me?"

"Partially because you didn't do it, and partially because he's your friend. I know jurisdictions that have gone to trial on a lot less than they have on you. Your car. You standing over the body. Gun in *your* purse. *Your* ex-husband."

"Great," I said. "I've heard enough. That's just great." Bryan pulled to the back of the historical society where reporters were swarming all over. "Maybe I should drop Aiden off right at school. I don't know how you'll navigate with these guys blocking your path."

"Oh! Aiden is staying with me today."

Bryan opened his door and then stuck his head back in the car. "Let me walk you in. Maybe I can dissuade some of these paparazzi from bothering you."

"I doubt it, but you can give it a try."

Bryan opened my door and before I even had both feet on the ground, the questions began. "Ms. Lockharte, did you kill Eddie Keeley?"

I looked at the man, and because he called me Ms. instead of Miss, I answered him. "No, I did not. I had nothing to do with it except finding him in my car."

Bryan pushed toward the door of the historical society, pulling me and Aiden and Bingo with him. When he got us inside, he said, "You should probably consider having a press conference to get rid of these guys, but you need to check with Billy boy and me to make sure what you say is acceptable and won't hurt you later."

"*Sheriff* Billy! Not Billy boy!"

"Okay, Aiden, okay. Sheriff Billy." Bryan rolled his eyes to me. "Tough kid." Bryan stopped before we got to the front. "Well, I'm going to drive to Phoenix now to pick up your car."

"How are you going to drive two cars home?" asked Aiden, who always got right to the point.

"I'll drive a loaner down there and leave it."

"What's a loaner?" Aiden wanted to know.

"A car that I'm borrowing. I'll leave it down there, and

the company who owns it will drive it back up here. Either that, or the car that I drive down there will be one that someone *else* left up here, and it belongs in Phoenix." He smiled at Aiden, hesitated, and then continued. "Lorry, Aiden, I will see you both later. Bye!"

We heard the door close behind him while we walked to the front. Petra was already in. "Hey, Petra. Did you already open?"

"No, why? Are we opening today?"

"Yeah, why not? I don't think those vultures will dare come over here after Billy warned them." I stepped into my office, turned the sign to *Open*, and unlocked the door. Across the street, I saw the reporters still gathered with their long-lensed cameras pointing right at me. "Aiden, would you color in here at Mommy's desk for a while? I want to talk to Petra."

"If someone comes in can I greet them?"

"Sure thing, kiddo!" After ruffling his hair, I bent down to pat Bingo and walked back to Petra's office. Sitting down at the chair by her desk, I leaned over so I could talk quietly. She leaned forward to hear. "Guess what Aiden and I woke up to today?"

"What?" she asked expectantly.

"Someone scrawled 'murderer' on our front door in dripping red paint."

"Does Billy know?"

"Yeah, he's there now, gathering evidence. I doubt if he'll find anything, though." Shaking my head, I looked at her. "Billy thinks the murderer did it, but I think he's wrong. I'm pretty sure I know who did it."

"Who?"

"You know that woman who was in yesterday? The one who almost kicked Bingo? Her name is Renee Croft.

93

I believe she did it."

"*That* was Renee Croft? She's the one who killed your sister, isn't she?" Petra asked.

CHAPTER TWENTY-ONE

"THAT'S A *RUMOR*, Petra. Where did you hear about it, anyway?" When my sister Lauren was a senior in high school, she and her boyfriend, and Renee Croft and her date, were driving together in a car that ultimately had a serious wreck. My sister and her boyfriend were sitting in the back seat, and Renee and her date were in the front. When the ambulance arrived at the scene, Renee was sitting in the back with Lauren, and Lauren's boyfriend was half in and half out of the driver's seat.

"But you believe it, don't you?" Petra looked at me.

I looked down and nodded my head. "Yes, I believe it." Why would the two girls be sitting in the back and Lauren's boyfriend driving when it wasn't even his car? Nobody could explain that, but nobody tried, either. Renee never got accused of the crime because her story never varied: she was in the back seat when the car crashed. And her date, whose car it was, ended up with brain damage and couldn't remember who was driving. He could barely remember who *he* was. I sighed. "But it was never proven. There was no way to prove it."

"Renee is a big girl. She could have easily carried the

boy—no matter how big he was."

"Yeah. She's a gymnast. Renee could probably lift a building if she wanted to."

"I'm sorry, Lorry."

I shook my head. "Long time ago, Petra. Long time ago."

The bell on the front door jingled, and the door opened. I heard Aiden say, "Good morning! Welcome to the Rutledge Historical—oh, it's you. Hello, Sheriff Billy."

Billy used to be one of Aiden's favorite people, probably second only to me and maybe Lily. It was sad that this situation had separated them like this. But I couldn't blame Aiden for feeling upset with the man who had put his mother in jail. In fact, his mother was upset with the man who had put her in jail—and I wasn't sure how soon I'd get over that.

"Aiden, I wanted you to know that I am giving a talk on bullying at your school today. So, hopefully, you won't have any more trouble. But if you do, just do what I told you. Do you remember?"

"I already did it!"

"Good job. That's my man! Is your mom here?"

I heard Aiden get off his chair and could imagine him standing there with his arms crossed when he answered, "What do you want with her?"

Petra and I looked at each other and both of us stifled laughter. "I'm in here, Billy."

"You haven't come to arrest her, have you?" Aiden said in a demanding voice.

"No, Aiden, I told you I won't do that." Billy walked into Petra's office. "Tough kid," he said softly.

"You're the second person today who's said that. He

protects his mommy. I like that."

"Fine," said Billy, sounding annoyed. But I knew he felt hurt with Aiden rejecting him like that.

I looked at Billy and squinted at his face. He had a couple of white spots—one on his cheekbone and one on his chin. "What are those spots?" I touched his face with my finger and thumb pointing them out.

He brushed my hand away and said, "Nothing. A bad face washing, I guess. Can you look at these pictures now?" He handed me his iPhone, and I saw a few more spots on his hands, but ignored them. Whatever they were.

"You took pictures with your iPhone?" I took the phone and began scrolling to see the pictures.

"What else? I was in my civvies, like you said."

"No. No. No. This one has possibilities, but it's only his back. Do you have another one of his front?" I held up the iPhone to Billy, but he shook his head from side to side.

"Couldn't. He disappeared after I took that, and I couldn't find him again."

I kept scrolling through the pictures. There were a lot of them, but except for the one guy's back, nobody else looked familiar. Handing him back his phone, I said, "Dead end, Billy. I guess I'll have to take matters into my own hands."

"What? What do you mean into your own hands?"

"It's obvious, Billy. If *someone* doesn't find the real murderer, then"—I mouthed the rest so Aiden wouldn't hear me—"you'll have to arrest me." Back in my normal voice again, I said, "And I can't let that happen." I shook my head and crossed my arms over my chest.

"Oh, no! You're not going there alone!"

"Do you have any idea how many times I've been in that casino alone looking for Eddie? A ton. More times than you have hairs on your head."

I must have pushed one of Billy's hot buttons, because he self-consciously took off his Smokey Bear hat and ran his hand through his hair. It looked thick to me.

"But not looking for these hoodlums, who might be Eddie's murderers."

"Well, then, what do you suggest, big guy?"

Billy scrunched his mouth and shook his head. "Let's go together. If you see them, you can discreetly point them out to me."

Still with my arms across my chest, I said, "Fine."

Billy motioned with his head to the other room. "What about *him? He* can't go to the casino. Who will babysit?"

Petra raised one arm in the air. "*I* will! Mason is coming down from Flag, and we'll be more comfortable at your house instead of mine, anyway."

Flag is what the Arizona locals call Flagstaff. And no, we don't call Phoenix *Phi.* Down there is "officially" referred to as *the valley.* Of course, where does that leave Verde Valley, since it is technically a valley, too? I don't know! I can't be expected to know everything, ya know!

"Sounds good. Petra, you and Mason want pizza for dinner? I'll have one delivered over there. And do you need to go home first, or can I drop you off at Lorry's?"

"I don't need to go home. I'll call and let my mom know. Pizza sounds good. Double pepperoni."

"Oh! I'm so embarrassed! I forgot to thank you for the pizza that you had sent over last night! Thank you so much! It was delicious!"

Billy looked puzzled. "What pizza?"

My mouth dropped open and the color ran out of my face. "Oh, no."

Billy acquired a huge grin on his face. "Gotcha!"

"Billy! That wasn't nice! Not with someone writing murderer on my front door!"

He looked down. "Yeah, you're right. I'm sorry. I guess I was trying to lighten the mood."

"Lighten the mood? When little ole me is the only viable suspect in a murder? Come on."

"All right. Sorry. I'll pick you up at five, drop Petra and Aiden off, and we'll go out for a nice dinner and then case the casino."

"Oh! Wait a minute! I'm getting a new car today. Let's take that. We can't go in your patrol car, anyway. It would scare off all the bad guys."

"Yeah, I guess you're right. But I get to drive."

"Drive my new car before *I* get to drive my new car? There ain't no way in Rutledge that I would let that happen. That's something Eddie would have done."

"Well, pardon me for asking to do something that *Eddie* would have done."

"Yeah, you better watch your step, or I might have to kill you, too." I said it softly so Aiden couldn't hear, but Billy and Petra could hear every word. Petra laughed.

Billy leaned forward and whispered, "Lorry! Don't ever say that! If anyone else besides me and Petra heard that—"

I shrugged my shoulders and tilted my head to the side. "I was just trying to lighten the mood."

Petra laughed again, and Billy stalked out without so much as a goodbye to any of us.

CHAPTER TWENTY-TWO

I SHOULD HAVE been happy and excited about going out to dinner with Billy—I had been wanting that for months. But, this, alas, was *not* a date. It was a business meeting. So there was no reason for me to get excited about it, anyway. Which was sad, really. Everybody seemed to think Billy was interested in me. Even *I* thought he was interested in me. But he had done nothing about it in all these months. And now the murder and all the bad feelings that had come with it.

Petra was still laughing when I walked into my office to get Aiden to move. But he had left the unfinished coloring page on the desk, and he was lying on his stomach on the floor propped up with his elbows and with his head on his hands, reading.

"Did you and Sheriff Billy get into a fight, Mommy? He seemed mad when he left. He didn't even say goodbye to me."

"No, not a fight, honey. Actually, I'm going out to dinner with him tonight, and Petra will babysit you."

"Petra?"

He jumped up and ran into Petra's office. When I

followed him in, he was holding her hands and jumping up and down, saying "Petra! Petra! Petra!"

"And Mason's coming, too, Aiden!" Petra smiled at Aiden.

"Mason! Mason! Mason!" Aiden cried.

"Okay, sweetie. Go back to your book and let Petra get her work done. Mommy needs to get some work done, too."

"I'm almost finished with the book. Can we go to the library like you promised?"

I nodded. "When you finish."

As I sat down at my desk, a couple walked into the room, setting the bell a-jingling. "Hello. Welcome to the Rutledge Historical Society. Can I help you?" I usually didn't say that, but it sounded good when Aiden said it, so I copied him.

"We'd like to look at the exhibits," said the man.

He and his wife were older, both of them with graying hair, but both dressed well in stylish clothes and expensive shoes. I showed them to the back where the exhibits were and returned to my desk. Aiden was once again lying on the floor reading with Bingo snuggled up on one side of him and Rocky the cat on the other.

A few minutes later, Aiden curled his legs beneath him and closed his book. "I'm finished, Mommy. Can we go now?"

"I haven't even had a chance to turn my computer on. Can we wait a little while? You can color a little longer, can't you?" I turned the computer on.

"No. No more coloring. I'm bored. I want to read."

There was rarely a time when Aiden *didn't* want to read. Swiveling my chair toward him, I said, "It's not that much fun being away from school, is it?"

"No. And Sheriff Billy said he was going to fix it. Can I go back now?"

"You can go back tomorrow."

"Okay," he said dejectedly. "Can we go to the library now?"

"I'll watch the place, Lorry. No worries. Go get the kid a book!"

"Yes, Petra, thank you. I'll go get the kid a book!" Petra, despite being a kaleidoscope girl, was great fun to work with. You never knew what she would come up with next. "Come on, kid."

I grabbed Bingo's leash, slipped it on him, took Aiden's hand, and we walked out the front door. Immediately, I knew we should have tried to sneak out the back. The reporters descended on us like a hungry pack of wolves. Except wolves don't do that—at least not in North America. There has never been an account of a wolf attacking a human except wolf-hybrids who don't count or wolves with rabies, who don't count either. That piece of trivia didn't make me feel any better, because the reporters weren't wolves, and I knew they were out for blood.

"Did you kill him, Lorry? Was it because he had a new girlfriend?" The man stuck a microphone in my face.

It was obvious that Renee had been talking. While I wondered what else she had told them, I kept my mouth closed and the three of us walked steadily toward the library.

"Was it jealousy because he had someone new and you have nobody?"

Well, at least now I knew what else Renee told them. I ignored them and kept walking. Aiden held tight to my hand with both of his, and Bingo stayed as close to me as he dared. Then Bingo yelped. One of the crowd of reporters pressing in had stepped on Bingo's foot.

Aiden suddenly broke away from me and looked up at the reporters with his tough guy stance—his arms crossed on his chest and his brows furrowed. "Now listen. All of you." He pointed his finger around the ring of reporters surrounding us. "My mommy didn't kill anyone. And I don't want you going around and saying that she did. That's slander, and it's illegal. And if you print anything like that, then it's libel. That is illegal, too. And if any of you step on my dog's toe again, I will kick you in the shin! *And* I'm under eighteen, so there is absolutely *nothing* you can do about it!"

He lifted his little foot into the air—he was flexible, too —and showed it to the reporters, who were snapping pictures like crazy. "I have my Van's on now, but I'm getting cowboy boots like Sheriff Billy, and if I kick you, it will hurt! But you hurt my dog! And I won't tolerate that!" He put his foot back on the ground, leaned down, and picked up each one of Bingo's four feet and kissed each one. Then he stood back up. "Now back off, go away, and leave us alone, or I'll tell Sheriff Billy that you're harassing us!"

The reporters, probably never having seen a seven-year-old go ballistic like that *and* quote the law to them, backed off. Aiden stretched out his arms in front of him and turned in a circle while motioning go away with his hands like he was shooing away a stray dog. I could still hear the click of camera shutters but no one said a word, and the crowd on the sidewalk in front of us split like Moses parting the Red Sea making it easy for us to move forward. As we walked away from them, I couldn't help myself patting Aiden on the shoulder and saying, "Good job, son."

The public library in Rutledge was on the corner of High Street just down from the historical society, so we didn't have far to go. It was an old two-story red brick building with ornate white wooden decorations on it, including two columns on the second story surrounding an arched stained glass window of a frog. No one ever knew what the frog had to do with reading, but in its defense, it did have a book in its little front feet. But you couldn't read the title of the book, so there was no way to know which way the frog's taste ran.

The building sat back from the sidewalk, so the front area was like a brick-lined patio. The red bricks on the patio did their best to match the bricks on the building, but they were much newer. A redwood bench and a white metal patio table and two chairs sat on the patio. Occasionally, you would see people out there reading books, but mostly it was old people who stopped to rest in the chairs on their way walking by.

We walked toward the library with the reporters following at a safe distance. They must have been afraid of Aiden's threat of wearing cowboy boots next time he saw them. Once inside, I thought we'd be *safe*, but that was too much to hope for. The librarians, Brandi and Catherin, knew us and greeted us warmly, but there were a couple of patrons who pointed and whispered behind their hands. This business of being accused of murder was no fun at all.

CHAPTER TWENTY-THREE

AS SOON AS we stepped through the door, Aiden ran across the floor, pushed into the swinging gate that separated the librarians from the rest of the library, and jumped into Brandi's arms. Brandi was a strange girl, twenty-five years old, somewhat of an airhead, and always dressed in black and white as if her real ambition was to work in a casino. She was also the head librarian.

Catherin was the other librarian. I watched as she frowned when Brandi swung Aiden around. When Aiden and Brandi finished their mutual admiration hug, Aiden gently and politely gave Catherin a more dignified hug. And he kissed her cheek. But the whole thing was brief before Catherin pulled away and gave him a pat on the behind to encourage him out through the swinging gate. "Go on. Out of here now!"

At first glance, you'd think she didn't enjoy it, but there was a hint of a smile on her face when he hugged and kissed her. Before I noticed that, I once asked Aiden why he insisted on hugging her when she acted like she didn't want him to. He said it was important to be kind to unkind people, because they needed it more.

Apparently he had gotten that off the internet at some point.

Catherin was in her early thirties, same as me, but she looked and acted much older. She dressed in unfashionably long skirts and blouses buttoned up to the top button. Her clothes were always dark colors and not very becoming. I could teach her a thing or two about clothes—and first would be to get rid of those ugly white nurse's shoes. Even nurses don't wear those shoes anymore. Catherin used to be the head librarian, but she was sick so often that the city finally gave the job to Brandi, who, when Catherin was around still let her boss her around. I wasn't sure whether I should admire Brandi or feel scorn for her for doing that. But it worked for them, so I supposed it was a good thing.

Aiden loved the library, and only being allowed two books at a time enabled him to hang out there more often. It used to be only one, but after a couple times when he finished the book on Saturday evening and panicked when the library wasn't open on Sundays, I insisted on him getting two—one for an emergency. It didn't matter that his bookshelves were filled with books —he knew what he wanted to read next and wouldn't settle for anything else. But after I suggested that he choose more than two today so we wouldn't have to endure the reporters again, he picked out several books to read.

When we left the library with Aiden carrying four books in his arms, the reporters swarmed around us again. Aiden stepped out in front of me and Bingo. "Leave us alone or I'll call Sheriff Billy! I mean it! Stop harassing us! My mommy is innocent!" He swung around and pointed his finger—best as he could with his arms full of books—at the reporters. "Back off!" Then he led the way down the street with me and Bingo following.

Knowing Aiden's picture would most likely show up on the front page the following day, I wondered how he would respond to it. Would he like the notoriety or be embarrassed about it? I'd probably find out soon enough. We walked into the historical society, and I felt great relief when we closed the door behind us.

Aiden put his books on the desk and rubbed his hands together in a downward clapping motion. "I took care of them! A man's gotta do what a man's gotta do."

I leaned down to talk to him. "Aiden, where did you learn about libel and slander and being under eighteen?"

He looked at me and blinked. "One time when Sheriff Billy and I went fishing, we talked all about that. And then I got a book about it at the library, so I could study it more. Why, Mommy? Shouldn't I have told them that?" It looked like tears were gathering in his eyes.

"No, baby, no! What you did was perfect! You protected your mommy and Bingo! It was awesome!" I picked him up, swung him around, and set him back down on the floor.

"Thanks, Mommy." With a smile on his face, he picked up one of his books, walked into Petra's office, sat down on the chair in front of her desk, and began reading.

I followed him in and Petra raised her eyebrows. Then she looked at Aiden, tapped on the desk in front of him, and said, "What was that about, Aiden?"

"Oh, nothing, Petra. I had to protect Mommy and Bingo. That's all." When Bingo, who had settled at Aiden's feet, heard his name, his tail thumped the floor.

"Sheriff Billy said I had to stand up for myself, so I figured I had to stand up for Mommy and Bingo, too." He returned to his book without another word.

Petra winked at me, and I retreated into my office, where I checked my email. On my desk was a folder of typing that must have been delivered while Aiden and I were at the library. I was about to start typing when Petra called out to me.

"Hey, Lorry. What was in that envelope that your mother's attorneys sent?"

"Oh! I forgot all about it." I pulled the envelope out of my top desk drawer and held it in my hand, not really wanting to open it. But now was as good a time as any, so I opened the clasp and pulled out the inside envelope. All the messages I received from the attorneys arrived in a messenger envelope with a white envelope inside. Sealed. I opened the white envelope and pulled out the neatly typed letter.

CHAPTER TWENTY-FOUR

THE LETTER IS the one that Bryan had mentioned. I had forgotten all about it—probably because I wanted to. Picking it up, I took a deep breath and read it aloud to Petra.

"Dear Ms. Lockharte, It has come to our attention that the threat of your returning to your former husband, Edward Keeley, has been negated. It is no longer in your best interest that we monitor your life and keep possession of the money that is rightfully yours. Therefore, the bulk of your mother's fortune will be transferred into your name. Please contact us with financial information so that the transfer can take place expediently. Sincerely—"

"Wow! The bulk of your mother's fortune! Wow! How much is it? Do you even know?"

"I have no idea, but I know it's a lot."

"Will you and Aiden be moving back into the Lockharte mansion, then?"

"What? *No!* That place is *huge*! I'd need servants just to keep it clean. Aiden, Bingo, and I would get lost in there. I love our little red gambrel house, and I have no plans to leave it."

The bell on the door jingled and someone came in the

door. I dropped the letter on the top of my desk and looked up to see who it was.

"Who are all those people outside?" asked my cousin Kasey.

"Reporters."

"They still think you did it?"

I shrugged. "Billy hasn't found the culprit yet. What else are they going to think?"

"You seem to be pretty calm about it."

"Yeah, well. Nothing else I can do right now. Aiden and I just walked to the library, and Aiden had to scare them off. He did a good job, too!" I hoped Aiden was listening, but he probably wasn't. When he got involved in a book, a bomb could go off next to him, and he wouldn't hear it.

"You know, everyone at the cafe is talking about the murder! It's so exciting!"

When Kasey says "cafe" she means the Rutledge Koffee Korner Kafe, which is right next door to the historical society—part of the same building, actually. It had been divided years before. "And who do they think did it?" I asked.

"You, of course. They had mixed feelings until I told them that you said you were glad he was dead. That convinced them. And—"

"Kasey! You weren't supposed to tell that to anyone! You promised!"

"Um, I don't remember promising!" She shrugged. "Sorry."

"Kasey, I can't believe you did that. What else did you tell them?"

Ignoring my question, she said, "So have you picked out a car yet?" She didn't give me a chance to answer, she just continued on. But I was used to that. "Because John did a lot of research on the RAV4, and it's a great car. And I wanted to suggest to you some extras you should get on it. Air conditioning, of course. Power windows, brakes. Child proof locks. I don't know about Aiden, but Lily would run out in the middle of traffic if she could. And you should get one of the upgraded colors as well. They have some pretty ones out now. Leather seats would be awesome. And—"

I hated to interrupt her, but she was annoying me with her constant chatter. Of course, she usually did that, anyway. "Kasey! Stop! I already gave Bryan what I wanted. Including heated seats. He's down in Phoenix right now picking it up."

"Heated seats? It's Arizona. What do you need heated seats for?"

"Because my butt is so big that it's like an extra appendage, and it loses heat quickly. I like my butt to be warm." The phone rang. "Just a minute, Kasey." I turned around to answer the phone. They wanted to know what the hours were and if we were open on the weekends. We're not. Just Monday through Friday. When I turned back to Kasey, she was leaning over my desk reading the letter from my mother's attorneys.

I felt a bad feeling in the pit of my stomach. She didn't even realize I was watching her, until I grabbed the letter out from under her watchful gaze.

"Lorry! Congratulations! You're getting all that money you thought you'd never get! Not piecemeal like you've been getting—a little for the divorce, the adoption, the house—now you get it all. How cool is that!"

Slowly, I stood up and put both my hands on her shoulders. "Kasey, I want you to swear on your marriage

111

that you will not tell another soul about this." I knew how much Kasey loved her husband and valued their marriage, so I thought if I said that she would take it seriously.

"Um, yeah, sure, okay. Of course I won't."

"Kasey! That's what you said when I asked you not to say that I was glad Eddie was dead." I gave her shoulders a little shake. Muscle memory. I thought she might remember it better that way. "Kasey, this is important. If the press gets hold of this, they'll go nuts with it. It will be front-page news!"

"Well, they won't get hold of it if you keep it in your desk."

"Kasey! I don't mean that! I mean if *you* spread it all over town! Please shut up about it!"

She smiled uncomfortably. "Oh, come on, Lorry. I don't talk *that* much."

Kasey rarely *stopped* talking. "Yes, you do! You told everyone at the Koffee Korner about what I said before. I can't have that!"

"Put duck tape on her mouth!" shouted Petra from the other room.

"It's *duct* tape, and that's not reasonable."

"Lorry, sorry, gotta go. See you later."

"Goodbye, Kasey," I said resignedly. As she walked out the door, I thought how sad it was that Aiden wouldn't be on the front page after all. His "protecting his mommy" bit would be usurped by my mother's fortune. And it would make me look guiltier than ever.

CHAPTER TWENTY-FIVE

"LORRY, THAT LETTER is so personal. I can't believe she would tell people at the cafe about it."

I stood just inside Petra's office. "That's typical Kasey. She told people that I said I was glad Eddie was dead. That's personal, too, don't you think?"

"Yeah, but that letter! She can't be that stu—"

"Don't call my Aunt Kasey stupid, Petra. That's not polite." Aiden looked up from his book, narrowed his gaze at Petra, and then returned to his book. He had been so quiet, we had forgotten he was even there. Aiden had a discriminating sense of propriety.

Petra made an oh-my-goodness face and shrugged. "Sorry, Aiden. I lost my head. I won't do it again. But isn't she your cousin, not your aunt?"

"Yeah, but I like to call her aunt. It makes her feel good."

"I'll have to wait and see if she does it," I said. "There's nothing I can do about it now besides stuffing a sock in her mouth—and she'd just take it out."

"Like I said"—Petra snuck a quick glance at Aiden —"duct tape."

113

I nodded. "That would probably be the only way to keep her quiet." I returned to my office and started typing.

The afternoon wore on and at three o'clock, Bryan came in the back door. Before he even got to my office, he announced, "Come see your new car! It's beautiful!"

Aiden, with Bingo at his heels, was the first one to run to the back. "Where is it, Bryan? Is it like yours?"

"Sorry, big guy, it's the one your mom wanted. Come out and see it though. I think you'll like it."

They were out the back door before Petra and I had a chance to walk there. When we stepped out the door, Aiden was standing there looking at the car and jumping up and down. "It's blue! I didn't know it would be blue!"

Looking at the car made me smile. It was indeed a pale blue. I had told Bryan that I wanted a light color—you know, because of the Arizona sun. And pale blue fit the bill. She was a beauty.

"It's beautiful, Lorry!" Petra walked around the car admiring it.

"Come on, get in!" Bryan opened the door for Aiden, and he climbed into the back seat. Then Aiden opened the opposite door, let himself out, and climbed into the front.

"I ride shotgun!" Aiden said as he bounced up and down on the seat. Glancing briefly at me, he climbed over into the driver's side, put his hands on the steering wheel, and pretended he was driving.

"Aiden, you know you can only do that when the car is parked and turned off, right?" I had heard of kids accidentally sliding the car into gear and rolling down the street. I'd have to remember to always put the parking brake on. "And you won't be riding *shotgun* for a few more years." Wherever does he get those expressions?

"Yes, Mommy, and I won't touch any of the gadgets on the dashboard or here." He pointed to the console where the shift lever was.

"Good man," said Bryan. And then to me, "So what do you think, Lorry? Does it meet your expectations?"

"It's perfect, Bryan. Thank you." I gave him a spontaneous hug, but I think it embarrassed him.

"Ah, you're welcome. Say, can you give me a ride to my car? It's on the other side of the bridge not too far from here." He took a step backwards. "But if it's too much trouble, I can catch a cab. No problem."

"Yes, of course I'll give you a ride." I turned to Petra. "Can you take care of the place for a while? And watch Aiden?"

"I want to go with you, Mommy!"

"I'm sorry, Aiden, I need to talk to Bryan about something."

"About Aunt Kasey talking too much?"

Even when he was reading, the kid didn't miss a thing. Sometimes a bomb could go off and he wouldn't hear it. At other times, he could hear a whisper in the next room. "Yes, sweetheart, among other things. You'll get to ride in it when we go home this afternoon. All right?"

Aiden climbed out of the car, stuck his hands in his front pockets, and looked at his shoes. The kid had a knack for looking extremely cute. But I think he was trying more for the pathetic look so I'd feel sorry for him and take him with me. "Yeah, I guess so," he said without looking up.

Petra, Aiden, and Bingo disappeared into the building, and Bryan and I stepped into the car. I adjusted the seat, put my hands on the steering wheel, and squirmed my butt around to get it comfortable in the leather seat. The dashboard was concise, but had everything I needed. It had a CD player and a USB connection for an iPod. It also had a phone connection for hands-free calling.

"Is it comfortable enough for you?" asked Bryan. "The seat moves up and down as well as forward and back."

"Yes, it's fine. It's perfect! Thanks so much, Bryan! I love it!"

I started it up and she purred like a kitten. Thinking that thought though, brought my allergies back, and I sneezed.

"I hope you're not allergic to your new car!"

"No, but the way it started up made me think of a cat, and I *used to be* allergic to cats."

"Sounds like you still are!"

"Yeah, well, it's taken me longer than I expected to get myself over that." I put the car in gear, started backing out, and then stopped. "Shoot. I forgot my purse! Oh, well, it's not far."

"No," said Bryan. "Not with your precarious legal position right now. That's all we need is for you to get arrested for driving without a license." He put his hand on the door. "I'll go get it."

Just then, Aiden popped out of the back door, holding out my purse. He walked over to the car window, and I held the button to roll it down.

"Petra said you'd need this."

"Thanks, Aiden. And tell Petra thank you, too."

Aiden returned to the door of the building. As he opened it, he turned around and gave me one of his disarming smiles. Man, that kid was cute! And sweet.

And kind. And smart. How lucky I was to have him. I felt grateful for that every single day.

"Bye, Mommy!" he said from the door as he waved. "I love you!"

"Love you, too! Be back soon!"

"That's a nice kid you've got there, Lorry."

"Don't I know it." I pulled out of the parking lot, drove down the alley and onto Bridge Street.

It wasn't until we were driving over the bridge that one of us spoke. It was Bryan. "What's this about your cousin talking too much?"

I sighed and snuck a quick glance at him before looking at the traffic in front of us. "You wouldn't believe what accidentally happened. You know that letter you said I'd be getting?" He nodded, and I continued. "I didn't open it until today. And I left it on my desk in plain sight. Kasey came in, and I didn't think anything of it. Then I got a phone call, and I turned away to answer it. While I was on the phone, Kasey read the letter and then commented on it." I closed my eyes briefly and shook my head. "Immediately, I knew I was in trouble. I made her promise not to say anything, but she's one of those people who can't help themselves.

"You know how you told me not to tell anyone that I hated Eddie enough to kill him? Well, I did something just as bad. I still felt upset when I went over to Kasey's house that day, and somehow I told her that I was glad that Eddie was dead. She spread that all over town even after I told her not to say anything about it. So there's no way she'll sit on this.

"Petra said the only way to keep her mouth shut was with duct tape, and I have to agree with her. Too bad I can't do it." Bryan chuckled at that, but said nothing.

"So—you think I'm in trouble?"

"Yes, I think you're in big trouble, but I don't think you should blame yourself or Kasey. That information—all of it—was bound to get out. This is a small town. People talk. That's just the way it is. That's why I live in Flagstaff. And although Flag is much bigger than Rutledge, that kind of talk still goes on. I think it's human nature."

"Well, what am I going to do about it now? It will probably be headlines in tomorrow's news."

Bryan nodded. "Yes, you're probably right about that. I think I'll have to pay Sheriff Billy a visit to get everything straightened out. Otherwise, he will probably be pressured into arresting you—for real this time."

CHAPTER TWENTY-SIX

WE RODE IN silence the rest of the way to the car rental agency where Bryan had parked his car. He stepped out of the car, closed the door, and stuck his head back in the window. "Listen, Lorry. Don't worry about it. I'll go see Billy tomorrow morning and get everything straightened out. Bye." When he pulled himself from the window, I closed it and started driving away. Then I looked back and saw him watching me go. He didn't look happy.

Although he said not to worry, how could I not worry? *He* looked worried! If I got arrested, what would happen to Aiden? The adoption wasn't final yet. The state could take him away from me and never give him back. And women's prison. That was too terrible to even think about. And Bingo! I'd barely gotten him back, I didn't want to lose him again. The reasons were mounting why I needed to find who killed Eddie. Taking a deep breath to calm myself, I guided the car over the bridge and into the alley so I could park behind the historical society.

When I walked into the society and unhooked the chain that designated for employees only, I could hear people talking softly in the exhibit section—including a louder child's voice. At least they weren't reporters. When I walked by Petra on the way to my office, she stopped me because of my hang-dog expression. "Hey, Lorry. What's wrong?"

"I told Bryan about the letter and about Kasey spreading it all over town, and he was worried. He said not to worry, but *he* looked worried. So now I'm worried." Sinking down in the chair in front of her desk, I sighed.

"You're feeling sorry for yourself, aren't you?"

"You always get right down to it, don't you, Petra?"

"Yup. So what's Bryan going to do about it? I know he'll do something."

"How do you know that?"

"Because that's the kind of guy he is. He gets things done. That's easy to see. So what is it?"

"Don't you get tired of always being right when you're only sixteen years old?"

She frowned at me and ignored the question. "So what's he going to do?"

"Oh, so now you're assuming that was a rhetorical question? Well, smarty-pants, it was!" I stood up and walked to the edge of the wall that separated her office from mine. "He's going to talk to Billy tomorrow morning."

I walked into my office with a smile plastered on my face so Aiden wouldn't know how upset I was. But he was a sensitive little bugger, and he usually knew when I was upset. He wasn't in the office, though. I glanced at the glassed-in gift shop next to me, and he wasn't in there, either.

Then I walked through the area where the historical

society exhibits were, passing first the schoolhouse exhibit with two old-time school desks, chalkboard with chalk and eraser, and the picture of a one-room schoolhouse. The next exhibit I passed was the clothing exhibit showing the little boy wearing a dress. Everyone got a kick out of that, especially the little girls—the boys, not so much. The voices got louder, and I could plainly hear that the one that was the loudest was Aiden's.

I shook my head. How could I have walked past the exhibit before and not been aware of my own son's voice? I felt so much like a terrible mother that I wanted to slap my face, but I didn't want Aiden or the visitors to hear the *smack*. So consumed by my misery, I hadn't even recognized Aiden's cute little voice.

Right there and then I decided that it couldn't go on like that. Except for my hour in the holding cell, nothing bad had really happened. Instead of worrying about bad things that might happen, I was going to practice—or at least I was going to try to practice—what I had once read about: *What if up* thinking. Instead of worrying what if I get thrown in jail? Or what if they take Aiden away from me? I will start thinking, what if they realize I'm innocent? What if I find Eddie's real killer? What if Sheriff Billy asks me out on a *real* date? I threw that last one in there, because I figure if I'm going to do it, I might as well do it all the way.

As I walked by the Grizelda's Bar exhibit, I heard Aiden giving the speech on the railroad that used to exist between Sedona and Rutledge. The exhibit had a picture of the railroad: a distant painting of one of the times it went over the bank, which was why they eventually removed it. The builders had dreams of connecting it to the Verde Canyon Railroad, which is still in existence today. But due to the Sedona–Rutledge train continually falling off the track, that idea had to be abandoned.

I didn't know all of this until Aiden told me about it, just like he was telling these visitors. One time he was in the office and had nothing to read, so I gave him the exhibits folder and he read all of it. All I had done was skim the folder, and I didn't know the material half as well as he did. And besides all of his other good qualities, he was a good little speaker, too. My boy. My *son*. He and I would stay together forever—or at least until he got married. I wouldn't really want to share my house with my daughter-in-law, whoever she might turn out to be. Although I knew Aiden would have good taste, so maybe it would be all right. Wait. No.

CHAPTER TWENTY-SEVEN

AS MUCH AS I wanted to stand there and listen to the rest of Aiden's talk about the remaining few exhibits, I didn't want him to catch me at it, because it might embarrass him. And there was no way I wanted to do that. Slowly, I tried to tiptoe back to the front. Have you ever tried to tiptoe in three-inch heels? I almost fell on my face, but caught myself in time. No scream or gasp or moan came from my mouth. Although I did bite my tongue. Ouch.

"Did you know he was doing that?" I asked Petra when I came to her desk.

"Yeah. I figured it would be all right. Aiden obviously knows how to take care of himself. He told me about the reporter incident."

"The *reporter incident*. Yeah. Sounds like a movie on HBO. If it wasn't for the *bulk of my mother's fortune* letter, it would probably be front page news. Maybe Kasey can keep her mouth shut for the rest of the day." I shrugged, looked up, and shook my head. "Well, I can dream, can't I?"

Walking the few steps to my office, I was about to sit

down when I thought of something and walked back to Petra. "Hey, do you remember if Billy said he would meet me here or meet me at home?"

"He said he would meet you here. Remember? He said he'd drop me and Aiden off at the house."

"Oh, yeah, but he's not driving now. I am. I wonder if that changes anything."

Just then, Aiden and the family he was giving a tour to approached from the back. Aiden was telling them about the Rutledge Koffee Korner Kafe and how it encroached, yes, he used that word, on the Rutledge Historical Society's building, and what poor taste he thought it was. I didn't teach him to say that. Honest. Although it was exactly how I felt. Do you think kids get that kind of stuff from osmosis? Yeah. Must be that.

Aiden led the family out and stopped at my desk. He spread his arm toward me, palm up, as if introducing me to a crowd and said, "This is my mommy, and she's—" He stopped talking and looked down.

I stood up to save him. "Hello, I'm Lorry Lockharte. I hope you enjoyed Aiden's presentation."

"Oh, it was wonderful," said the father.

"Very informative," said the mother.

The twin girls said, "And he's cute!" and then disappeared behind their hands and a multitude of giggles.

The whole family was dressed in jeans and hiking boots, which were dusty. They must have spent the day hiking and then come to the historical society afterward.

Holding up a five dollar bill, the father looked at me and raised his eyebrows in question. I nodded. Then the father held out the bill to Aiden and said, "This is a tip for a great tour!"

Aiden started to reach for the bill with a huge smile on his face and then drew his hand back. "I think the tours here are free, sir. I can't accept that money."

Then he looked at me, and I nodded to him in encouragement. "It's a tip, Aiden. It's okay for you to take it."

"Are you sure, Mommy? Because I don't want to break any rules." I nodded to him, and a smile crept back onto his face.

I'll have to give the man credit. When Aiden said he couldn't accept it, the man did not pull the bill back. He continued to hold it out there. Now he took a step forward to hand it to Aiden again.

"Thank you!" Aiden said, looking proud.

"You did a great job, Aiden," the mother said. "You deserve it!"

The twin girls, still giggling, slipped out the door behind their father. The mother followed and turned back to Aiden saying, "It was a great tour, Aiden. Really." She smiled at him, walked out, and closed the door.

Aiden stood on his tiptoes watching them pass the front window. As soon as they were gone, he jumped into my lap. "Mommy! They said I did great! I got a *tip*!" He waved the five dollar bill in front of me.

At that moment, Sheriff Billy stomped in from the back and stood there with his hands on his hips and a scowl on his face. "Who got a tip in here?"

Uncertainly, Aiden glanced at me and then stood up facing Billy. "I did. Here it is." Aiden held up the bill. "And it's a tip! I did not charge for the tour! This is perfectly legal." He turned around to look at me again, and I nodded.

"A tip, huh? So you gave a tour of the historical society?" When Aiden nodded, Billy continued. "And they must have thought you did pretty well if they gave you a tip, huh?"

Feeling more confident, Aiden set his jaw and said, "They said I did *great*."

Billy took his hands off his hips and left them at his sides. "Then I guess there's only one thing I can do about that." He leaned over and swept Aiden off his feet and into his arms. "Give you a great big hug to congratulate you!"

I knew that ever since Aiden had snubbed him when this whole murder thing started, Billy had felt bad about it. Billy missed their closeness and the affection. When Aiden put his arms around Billy's neck and squealed with joy, I knew Aiden had missed Billy, too. It was good to see them together again.

Billy put Aiden on the ground and kneeled so that he was at eye level with him. "What are you going to do with all that money, little pard?"

"Well, I'd like Mommy to take it to the casino for me."

"You want us to put it in the slot machines for you? Quarter or dollar?"

Aiden laughed, not in an offensive way, but like he had never heard anything so silly. "No, of course not! Have you read the statistics on slot machines? A few people win, yes, but the casino has the advantage. I just want something out of the gift shop." He nodded his head. "You know—a sure thing!"

Billy stood up and smiled at Aiden. "Yeah, I bet you do! I should have known *you* weren't a gambler."

CHAPTER TWENTY-EIGHT

"ALL RIGHT, EVERYONE! It's five o'clock! Let's lock up and blow this pop stand!" Billy shouted.

"Let's blow this pop stand!" Aiden repeated as he jumped up and down still waving his five dollar bill. As adult as he often acted, sometimes I forgot he's still a kid. He's seven years old, and he is definitely still a kid. Then again, Billy started it.

"Here, let me take that, and I'll get you something cool." I took the bill out of his hand and put it into my purse.

Billy locked the deadbolt on the door, changed the sign to *Closed*, and led the way out back, with Aiden jumping up and down behind him, then Petra and me in the rear with Bingo on a leash. I guess that's because I'm bottom-heavy.

Petra locked the back door as Billy walked around my new car. "Nice car," he said. It was barely drizzling, but not enough to matter. We all ignored it.

"I want to sit with Sheriff Billy!"

"Sorry, little pard, I'm going to sit in front with your mom. You can sit in the back with Petra."

Aiden hopped over to Billy, looked up at him with his long lashes, and took his hand in both of his. "But you're going to the casino with Mommy, and I'm going to spend the evening with Petra. So you get to sit with Mommy then, and I can talk to Petra this evening. Wouldn't it make more sense if you sat in the back with me now?"

A broad grin spread across Billy's face. "I swear it. This kid's going to be an attorney!" Then he climbed in the back seat with Aiden, who looked triumphant. Looking in the rearview mirror, I noticed that Billy still had the two white spots on his face.

"Billy, what *are* those white spots?"

Billy tried to see himself in the rearview mirror, but couldn't, so he rubbed his hand over his face, found the two spots and tried to pick them off. "Nothing!"

Petra got into the front with me. "Can I drive, Lorry?"

"I didn't think you knew how to drive, Petra." I started the car and looked at her.

She smiled. "I don't. But this would be a great time to start!"

"Petra, would you like me to teach you to drive?" asked Billy from the back.

"Not in your patrol car!"

"No, not in the patrol car. Of course not. In my truck."

"Why doesn't Mason teach you to drive?" I asked. Mason was Petra's boyfriend. A handsome boy whom I used to define by his tattooed body until I found out he was in pre-med. Yes, I'm that shallow. Or at least I was. So sue me. Besides, I'm getting better.

"All he has is a motorcycle!"

"Petra, my truck is a stick. If you learned first on Mason's motorcycle, it would help you."

"I'll ask him."

By the end of that brief conversation, we had parked in front of my house, and we all exited the car. It was then I noticed my front door didn't have any writing on it anymore. The blood-red *murderer* had been repainted with white paint! When I glanced at Billy with a smile on my face, he sheepishly returned the smile and shrugged. Now I knew what the white spots on Billy were. We all went through my now clean front door into the house.

That morning I had dressed for the casino, but after seeing Billy out of his sheriff's uniform and wearing a fancy cowboy shirt with tan Levis that fit him tighter than they ought to, I thought I should dress in the same way. I took a deep breath as I followed his cute butt into the house. That man took my breath away. And it made me wish anew that tonight was pleasure and not business.

When I came out of the bedroom and into the living room, Billy looked me up and down and whistled. "Ya look real purty there, little lady."

I wore a layered denim skirt with a dark blue cowboy shirt with delicate white lace covering the light blue yolk. And high-heeled cowboy boots. That's probably what made Billy whistle. Petra looked at me and winked, and I looked away. This was strictly business, regardless of Billy's wolf whistle. He also had on a Stetson cowboy hat, but I didn't have one of those.

Billy put out his arm for me, and I slipped mine through it. Then he held the front door open, and we left the house. Mason wasn't there yet, and Billy had ordered the pizza to arrive at six o'clock to give him more time. Petra and Aiden had been sitting on the couch reading as we walked out the door. I knew Aiden was safe with

Petra and Mason, but every time I left that kid, I felt it in my heart.

"Sure I can't drive?" asked Billy as we approached the car. He held his arm over his head. The drizzle was about to turn to rain, as I watched the drops getting bigger and plopping onto the windshield. The fragrant smell of rain filled the air.

"Yup, I'm sure," I said as I slid into the driver's seat.

"Nice car. Nicer than your old one."

"Yes, it was kind and considerate of Eddie to get killed in it. He wrecked my first Taurus and died in my second one."

"Good choice then buying a Toyota. If you had bought another Taurus, he might have haunted it."

I nodded. "Probably."

It sounded stupid, but I wouldn't put anything past Eddie. If there was a way he could haunt me, then he'd do it. As I drove across the bridge toward Coyote Moon Casino, Billy leaned over to look at the dash. He turned the radio on and off, the heat, rolled the window up and down, and finally reached into the glove compartment, pulled out the Owner's Manual, and started reading it.

Then he leaned over to look at my steering wheel and without saying a word, he bent over, picked up my purse that was by his feet, and pawed through it. "What are you doing with my purse?" I couldn't believe he'd go through it without an explanation. No, that's not right. I couldn't believe he'd go through it at all.

"Just relax. You have Entune. I'll set up your hands-free cell phone for you." He proceeded to take my phone out of my purse and tapped around on it. Then he tapped around on the dashboard and when he finished that, he went back to tapping on the phone. "Okay. All set. Now let's test it." He reached over me and pushed a button on the steering wheel. "Call Petra!" he said.

"What?" I asked.

"Shhh!" he replied.

Suddenly, I heard Petra's voice over the car speakers. "Yes, Lorry, everything is fine. What do you need?" Petra asked in a bored voice.

"It's Billy, Petra! Can you call back? I'm testing something."

"Sure," I heard Petra say.

A second later Billy's cell phone rang, and he reached into his pocket to get it. "Petra! I meant call Lorry back! I'm setting up her bluetooth phone in her car."

"What's a bluetooth? Something a whale has?" I asked.

Next thing I knew, the car was making a funny sound and Billy pressed a button on the steering wheel. "Hey, Petra. Perfect! Thanks!" He pressed the steering wheel button again. "There ya go, Lorry. All set! All you have to do is press that button to answer and that button to hang up."

Billy pointed to two buttons on the steering wheel, one had an icon of a phone lifted *off* the cradle and the other had a phone with the handset *on* the cradle. You would have thought they could come up with icons using cellphones instead of the old-fashioned handset and cradle variety. But oh well. You can't have everything.

As in most cities, traffic was heavy around rush hour so I had time to tell Billy about Aiden's dealings with the reporters, and how he stood up for himself like Billy had taught him. Billy got a kick out of that—especially the part about getting cowboy boots like his.

"Do you know what size shoe he wears?" Billy asked.

131

"He's my son! Of course I know what size shoe he wears!"

Billy looked at the clock on the dash and said, "Turn at the light. I'm going to buy him some cowboy boots!"

I turned a couple of more times, and we parked in the back lot at Boot Barn. I had never been in there. Eddie wouldn't be caught dead in anything that resembled cowboy attire, which made me wonder what he had been caught dead in when I last saw him. Dead. In my car. In all the excitement, I didn't notice what he wore.

After running under the awning to avoid the now heavier rain, we walked in and the first thing we came to was a rack of clearance items, which I walked past without even looking. To the left was men's wear, to the right was women's wear, and straight ahead were boots. Children's boots were on the back wall.

Billy pulled up one pant leg and compared his boot to the different children's boots—medium brown with fancy stitching on the side and on the toe. He finally found one that looked exactly like his, so I grabbed the size two box. He opened the box, made sure they looked like what they were supposed to, checked to make sure there was a right boot and left boot, and then said, "If they don't fit, I'll bring Aiden to exchange them." Looking at me, he added, "If that's okay with you."

"Sure, Billy. I don't mind, and it would be a fun time for Aiden. But I think they'll fit. He just went from size one to size two, so they should be fine."

We checked out with the cashier and Billy paid for the boots looking proud of himself. "We'll have matching boots!" he said with a big grin on his face.

When we got back into the car, he sat in the passenger seat still admiring Aiden's boots, which were in his lap.

He looked down toward his pant leg, which was still rolled up. "They look just like mine! Same color and everything!" Holding one boot out in front of him, his smile faded, and he looked at me. "Do you think he'll like them?"

"Billy, he'll *love* them!"

With the boots back in the box, Billy sat there looking pleased with himself, so I thought it was time to tell him the story of the letter that Kasey saw and what I expected her to do with that information. When he heard it, he groaned. "That's what we don't need right now. But I'm meeting Bryan in the morning, and he's going to introduce me to the investigator who's been following you. Supposedly they have a video of your whole morning, which should clear you. At least I hope it will."

"Billy, you don't still think I did it, do you?" I couldn't believe he might still think that, but I had to ask. You know, to make sure of where I stood with him.

He put his hand on my shoulder and turned to face me, although it looked like his eyes were far away. A sharp bolt of lightning exploded in the sky. "Lorry, I never thought you did it. I had to be sure, because"—he looked down—"because—" But he never got to finish because the car phone rang. I looked at the steering wheel to see where to press. "Hello!" Although I had no idea why she would call again, I assumed it was Petra.

Then, from out of the speakers in my car, a voice shouted, "Murderer! Murderer! Murderer!" Before I could react or say anything, the person had hung up.

CHAPTER TWENTY-NINE

"OKAY, THAT DOES it!" said Billy. "When I talk to Bryan tomorrow, I'm going to ask him to keep the investigator taking video of you until this whole thing is settled, and maybe we can catch whoever's doing this." He shook his head and then shook his fist in the air. "This aggravates me so much! And it sounded like Darth Vader, so they used a voice changer. You can get a free one off the internet, so that's a dead end."

The whole thing gave me the creeps. Maybe Billy was right and I was wrong about the person who painted *murderer* on my door. I thought it was that thoroughly unpleasant woman, Renee Croft.

But now, with the phone call, maybe it really was Eddie's murderer. I shivered. Eddie's murderer out there targeting *me*. Maybe I was next. Maybe whoever was doing this held me accountable for one or all of Eddie's sins. And Eddie had a *lot* of sins. But he and I hadn't been together for months. In the scheme of things, though, several months isn't much. Even from the grave Eddie was a bother.

"Here we are," said Billy in a gruff voice.

"Hey, don't be mad at me! *I* didn't make the call."

"Oh, Lorry. I'm not mad at you. I'm only mad that I can't stop it from happening to you. Apparently, I'm not doing a very good job of protecting you."

"You're not my protector. I can take care of myself."

Billy shook his head and pointed to a parking place. His eyes got that faraway look again, and I wondered what he had been about to tell me before the phone call, but I felt like it was the wrong time to ask.

The parking lot was huge and wound around to the front of the casino. The Coyote Moon Casino looked like a huge hogan made of logs with a multitude of windows. The logs looked like they had mud in-between. I didn't know if it was real logs and real mud or make-believe logs and mud, but it looked real to me. When it was being built, the Native Americans supervising the construction had insisted that the front door face east, as it would in a traditional hogan. There were doors in each of the four cardinal directions—north, south, east, and west—but the main entrance was in the east, and that's where the valet parking was, too. They had also nixed the idea of a square entryway attached to the hogan, so a smaller hogan had been built next to the main one, but it was only a shell of a hogan creating an entryway.

Although the rain had stopped, the clouds still hung in the sky threatening more rain. After I had parked and turned the car off, Billy stepped out and shoved Aiden's new boots in under where his feet had been. He looked at me looking at him, and he shrugged. "It's a new car, and it's pretty. People are going to look in. This will keep the honest people honest."

We walked in under the partial shell hogan and the automatic doors opened for us. Immediately, the lights and sounds of the slot machines assaulted us. To be fair, it wasn't anything like it used to be. I had gone to a casino for dinner with my mother when I was in my teens, and that's when you used *real* money. So when someone won, it wasn't just the lights, bells, and whistles, but you could also hear the coins falling into the tray. I have to say that the sound made you want to try your own luck. Without the coins jangling down—not so much. Even if you were used to today's slot machine lights and sounds, it still felt overwhelming. Sad to say, I was once used to all these sights and sounds. And happy to say, since I left Eddie, I haven't returned to the casino at all until today.

It was amazing all the different kinds of slot machines designed to take people's money. That was their whole purpose in life. Back when I was married to Eddie, I used to know someone who had once worked in a casino, and she used to say the casinos didn't get that tall off people winning. Eddie, as much of a degenerate gambler as he was, at least never fell for the allure of the slot machines. I, on the other hand, never felt the allure, but when Eddie dragged me with him to the casino—which thankfully wasn't often but still too often for my liking—I sometimes sat in front of a machine killing time with pennies or nickels. Pennies could pass the time without much regret. But you wouldn't believe how fast you could lose ten or twenty dollars playing nickel slots— even using the minimum one nickel. Although I occasionally won, and I'll admit it was exciting and felt good, the main draw for me was the release from boredom.

Billy led the way through the casino past all the tourists and the black-and-white–dressed employees.

They always reminded me of penguins. When we got to the restaurant, he passed it by. I thought maybe he didn't realize it, so I tugged on his arm. He briefly put his arm around me to bring me with him. "Lorry! I know you're hungry, but let's walk by the poker room first. I don't want to miss them again."

I was hungry, too. All day I had been looking forward to having a buffalo burger. You wouldn't think someone like me would like such a thing, but I do. The first time I ever had one, Eddie literally forced me to try it. I can't remember what he promised me or more likely threatened me with, but I reluctantly ate it. And it turned out I loved it. That's what I would always have whenever we were here and Eddie won and sprung for dinner. But away Billy and I walked from the juicy buffalo burger. My stomach growled.

CHAPTER THIRTY

THE POKER ROOM was across the casino from the restaurant, through rows and rows of slot machines. We also passed the blackjack and weird-card game tables which were green quarter-circles. The dealer stood on the inside of the circle, and the chairs and the gullible patrons sat on the outside of the circle. I called them *weird* card games because there were always new ones that the casino dreamed up and where the gullible ones tried to win. Blackjack was different. If you knew the correct strategy, then your chance of winning against the casino was roughly one to one. If you could count cards, you had an advantage over the casino—over the long run, that is. And sometimes you could lose thousands before the cards went in your favor. That was the irony. If you knew how to play, the casino wouldn't let you play. When they caught card counters, they kicked them out and put them on a black list so they couldn't return.

The Coyote Moon poker room had six Texas Hold'em tables, which were long ten-person poker tables. They sat eleven people, the eleventh person being the dealer. Green felt covered the tables with the Coyote Moon insignia—a coyote howling at the moon—embossed on it. And around the perimeter of the table was a wide four or five inch strip of green molding with regular holes for drinks. They didn't want the wet drinks on the green felt, and the holders prevented *most* spilled drink accidents. Four of the tables were along the railing with two in the back. There was a counter at one edge of the room with a white board behind it listing the people who had signed up to play and were waiting for an opening. There was one bored person behind the counter, but no one on the list now.

The casino held tournaments on Monday afternoons and Thursday evenings, but the rest of the time, it was regular play. Hold'em was the main game, but they also played two variations called Pineapple and Omaha. Eddie had tried both of them and lost so bad that he took up betting sports with a bookie for a while after that. Of course, that didn't work out, either, so he eventually went back to regular Hold'em, where he occasionally won. Occasionally being the salient word. He fancied himself a professional, but he was a rank amateur, with the debts to prove it.

Billy stopped before we were in view of the poker room. From where we stood, we could see it, but no one in there would see us unless they were looking for us, because in our matching cowboy outfits we blended in so well with the slot machines. Or whatever. The table closest to us was filled with ten people playing and the dealer sitting in the middle spot on one side of the table. The table on the other side had a dealer and four people playing. Billy looked at me and raised his eyebrows in question. I shook my head. Neither of the two brutes who had come to our house was playing poker, and the two men outside the railing watching were not the bad guys, either.

"All right. Let's go eat. Then we'll check again. I hate to leave without finding them. How late can Petra stay?"

"Let's hope it doesn't come to that. I'm hungry. Let's go."

We turned around and retraced our steps. But as we headed toward the restaurant, we passed the Coyote Moon Gift Shop, and Billy dragged me inside.

"Come on! Let's get something for Aiden with his five dollars!"

"Okay," I said with all the strength I could muster on an empty stomach. It wasn't that I wasn't thinking of my boy and wanting to get him something cool. It was that I was starved.

The gift shop had the usual array of touristy stuff with the Coyote Moon logo on it: coasters, t-shirts, sweatshirts, and who knows what else. But since it was a Native American casino, there were also some genuine Native American items: Navajo rugs, beads, baskets, pots that looked like they came from the Anasazi or the Ancestral Puebloans, whichever you chose to call them. They were pretty cool.

"What would he want?"

"Something Native American. He likes that."

"How about this?" He stood in front of a rack of various small items, including necklaces, bracelets, Indian headbands, and dream catchers.

Billy held up a dream catcher, which Aiden would like, but it looked somehow wrong. I turned it over in my hand and saw why. "Look at this, Billy. Made in China." I picked out a bigger one, a more natural looking one, farther up on the rack. "This one. This one is real."

Billy looked at the prices. The one from China was $4.95 and the real one was $8.95. "Oh, come on. How is he going to know the difference? We'll take the tag off."

I stood there with my hands on my hips. "Billy, it's *Aiden*. Of course he will know the difference."

"I don't believe that. A dream catcher is a dream catcher."

I held both of them up. "Seriously, Billy. You can't tell the difference between these two? It's obvious. This one has real rawhide, and this one is made of fake stuff."

"But it's more than he can afford."

"*That* he won't know about. Like you said, we'll take off the tag."

"I still don't believe it," Billy said as we walked to the cash register.

"I'll tell ya what, Billy. If he doesn't mention how real it is, I'll give you five dollars. And if he does notice, you give me five dollars. Deal?"

He slapped my hand in agreement, I paid for the dream catcher, and we left the gift shop. Then we proceeded to the restaurant, Coyote Moon Buffet and Steak House. It was a pleasant restaurant protected from the din of slot machines by a glass barrier, but I knew from experience that it didn't shut them out entirely. Eddie and I would occasionally eat there when he had a winning day, which wasn't that often.

Billy and I sat at a table for two with a candle on the table. I was hoping the hostess wouldn't light it when we sat down, but she did. With that candle and the table for two, I could almost pretend that this was a *real* date instead of a business arrangement. I had just taken a sip of the ice cold water with lemon when Billy handed me a menu. As I looked up, I immediately put the menu in front of my face.

"Lorry? What are you doing?"

Moving the top of the menu toward him without revealing my face, I whispered, "It's them. They're sitting together three tables behind you."

CHAPTER THIRTY-ONE

BILLY SURREPTITIOUSLY LOOKED around the restaurant until he saw them and then kept looking all around at the restaurant so as not to be noticed. He leaned forward and whispered, "Stay right here and keep hidden behind the menu. I'll be right back." And just like that, he disappeared out the door.

I had told Billy that the two men were big and burly and mean, but now that I looked at them sitting at a dining table, looking normal, talking and laughing—not holding a gun in their hands—they didn't look so mean. They didn't look that big, either. Eddie was only five feet nine inches, so gauging by him, men who were taller than him were big. But Billy was six-four, so now I had another gauge. It was hard to see while the two men were sitting down, but I wasn't so sure they were any taller than Billy. What they were, though, was burly. They both looked like football players. What are the players who are as big as whales and push everyone else down? I couldn't remember and I didn't want to remember. Eddie always tried to teach me the *finer points of the game* as he called it. But apparently I wasn't a good student, probably because I didn't want to be. Anyway, these two men were as big as whales, but with solid muscle instead of blubber.

While I was sneaking glances at the two men, Billy had been busy. Just as the men's food arrived, Billy, accompanied by two security guards, marched up to their table. The two men looked surprised. I watched them scan quickly for the exits, but a security guard covered every one. With nowhere else to go, they stood up, and the security guards escorted them out with Billy in the rear. I watched them go wondering what I should do, but as they went through the door, Billy motioned me to follow. But I was starved! Color me hungry. *Very* hungry. I thought about ordering something to go and having it delivered to wherever they were going, but I didn't have time, and I didn't know where they were going, anyway. So I got up and dutifully followed, with my stomach growling so loud that it was competing with the noise of the slot machines. Almost.

It looked like a parade with me and Billy, the two hoods, and all the security guards walking through the casino. The ones who had been guarding the exits had filed in behind me, probably to watch whatever it was going on. But *I* didn't even know what was going on. When Billy and I had discussed coming down here, I didn't know he would make such a rigamarole about it. I thought he'd just talk to the men. If they did it, though, then it wouldn't have been such a good idea confronting them out in the open. When I thought it through that way, it made more sense.

We hadn't walked far through the casino when we turned off to a door that said *Employees Only*. It led down a passageway to the bowels of the casino. There was a huge contrast from the glitz and flashing lights above. Down here, the walls were dirty white in need of painting, and midway to the floor, there was a dark brown *bumper* of sorts to keep the wall from getting scratched and marked up. The bumper was scratched and marked up is why I say that. And it could also use a coat of paint. And to confirm my oh-so-not-educated guess, down the hall came one of those big cash trucks that they utilize to collect the money from the dealers, pushed by a black-and-white–uniformed employee. It whacked the wall—I mean the *bumper*—as it went by, on its way to the coin room.

Our parade came to a stop in front of a door that the leading security guard unlocked and led us through. It was a medium-sized room with two tables surrounded by four chairs each, and a coffee maker against a counter on the back wall. There was a couch with an end table on each side of it covered with dog-eared magazines. The room might have been a private break room for management. There was nothing fancy about it though. And it could use a fresh coat of paint like everything else I had seen down here out of sight from the public.

The security guard left, and I heard him lock us in, which frightened me. After Billy patted the two men down for weapons, they sat at a table with him. I sat at the other table. Now that they were away from the restaurant and not smiling anymore, they looked as mean as I had seen them in our house so long ago. One of the men looked at me and elbowed the other one. "Hey, Earl, it's Eddie's woman—the one he told us to kill."

"Yeah, that's her all right," said the other one.

Billy, horrified, looked at me, and I shrugged. Billy

tapped the table with the end of his fingertips. "Okay, gentlemen, let's get down to business. So, you have just confirmed that you knew Eddie Keeley."

"Yeah, we know him. What of it?"

"Where were you this past Monday morning?"

The one called Earl laughed. "Hey, Tony, should we tell him where we was on Monday?"

Tony didn't even smile. "We were in lockup."

"Where?" asked Billy.

"Here. Right here in C-Moon."

C-Moon was what some of the locals called Coyote Moon. It was an abbreviation that I never used even when I lived here.

"For what?" asked Billy.

"Assault with a deadly weapon. But the charges were dropped." Earl smiled an ingratiating smile.

Billy ignored it and nodded. "Yeah, I'll bet they were."

"What's this about, anyway?" asked Earl.

"Someone murdered Eddie Keeley on Monday morning."

Earl laughed again. "And you think *we* did it? That no-account loser still owes us money!"

"How much?"

Earl motioned to Tony who pulled a small notebook out of his pocket. He flipped through it, ran his finger down a page, and said, "Two thousand, three hundred forty-four dollars, plus interest."

"It wouldn't be the first time someone was killed because they owed money—to teach others a lesson," Billy said.

Earl laughed yet again. He must have thought Billy was a funny guy. "That pissant? Killing him wouldn't teach anybody a lesson except how not to be a jerk." He pointed to me. "Have you checked *her* out? I'm surprised *she* hasn't killed him long before this."

"This is about you two, not her. So you were both in lockup on Monday morning?"

"Yeah, we spent Sunday night there and were released late Monday afternoon. It should be easy to check."

Billy nodded. "Gimme your driver's licenses." He pulled out his cell phone and walked toward the coffee machine which was as far as he could get from us in the room. As he was mumbling into the phone, Tony asked, "So you stayed with him after he told us to kill you?"

"He didn't mean it," I answered without looking up.

"Of course he meant it," said Earl. "That's the kind of lesson we teach people—hurt someone they love. Eddie knew that and yet he left you alone with us. How could you stay with someone like that?" Apparently, even bad guys could have some compassion.

"I left him."

"After that happened?"

I looked down. "No, just a few months ago." The incident had happened a couple of years before, so I wasn't surprised when both men started laughing.

"Stop talking to her!" said Billy with his hand over his cell phone. "Leave her alone. She has nothing to do with you."

"Not any more she doesn't, since she left the loser!"

Billy walked back to the table and handed the men back their licenses. "It's verified. It couldn't have been either of you. Do you know who else might have wanted to murder Eddie?"

"Maybe one of the husbands of the women he chased after." Earl looked at me wondering if I knew. Unfortunately, I did.

"Eddie was not a nice guy, sheriff. It will not be easy to find out who killed Eddie Keeley. There are a lot of people who aren't at all sorry that he is dead." Tony looked at me. "Including *her*."

CHAPTER THIRTY-TWO

AFTER BILLY KNOCKED on the door to signal the security guard to unlock it, and after the two men left, Billy put his hands on my shoulders and looked into my eyes. "Is there something you want to tell me?"

I knew what he wanted: the story about Eddie telling the two hoods to kill me. What *I* wanted was food. I was famished, and I wasn't going to wait any longer. "Later, Billy. I need to eat."

Billy looked at his watch. "It's late already. Do you think we should head home?"

Sighing, I nodded after looking at my watch. "I don't know how long Petra can stay, and I don't want to keep her if she needs to get home."

"We could call her," Billy suggested.

"Let's just go. I'll come another time to get a buffalo burger."

Billy smiled. "Is that what you were going to get?"

Nodding, I said, "I love them. The first one was forced on me, and after that, I was hooked."

"All right, let's go. We'll pick up something on the way home."

149

"Maybe there's still pizza left." We emerged into the casino with the bright lights. Except for the buffalo burgers, if I never returned to this place, it would be more than fine with me.

Billy laughed. "Are you kidding? With Mason around? That guy could eat an entire cow by himself!"

When we walked outside, the pavement was already drying from the brief rain, and the clouds made for a beautiful sunset. Billy, pointing to the west and putting his arm casually around me, said, "Look at that. Isn't it beautiful?"

While I nodded and forced my head to stay upright, I thought about how sweet the moment was. It didn't feel like a business date. And my head wanted so badly to rest on Billy's shoulder, but unfortunately that was way too intimate for where our friendship stood—especially now with the murder investigation hanging over us. And a second later at the car, he pulled his arm away and slid into the passenger seat.

Still, the moment had made me feel grateful. If anything *did* ever come of our relationship—that is, if it ever became more than just friends—I was glad he was the kind of man who noticed sunsets. Because not all men did. Eddie never did. If I ever pointed one out to him, he usually never even looked, and if he did, it was because a good-looking woman was walking in front of it. But Billy was *nothing* like Eddie. Thankfully.

We went to a drive-thru for dinner, and Billy promised he would make it up to me sometime and get me a buffalo burger. I told him it wasn't necessary, but warned him not to get any grease on my new car. Then I dropped a French fry on my new leather seats and panicked, until Billy wiped it off with his napkin. It didn't leave a mark.

When Billy finished eating, he rubbed the napkin over his hands, patted his mouth, and put everything in the bag. Then he started going through my purse.

"Hey, what're you doing in there? Searching it for weapons—again?"

He held up the bag with the dream catcher in it. "Nope. Just looking for this. Unless you consider this a weapon."

"Only to nightmares!"

By that time, we were almost home because traffic was light later in the evening. Billy turned toward me, put his hand lightly on my shoulder, and asked me to tell him the details about those two thugs and Eddie telling them to kill me. So I told him in detail everything that had happened, what was said, and what Eddie did. And I told him how hard my heart was beating afterward, and how bewildered I felt that Eddie had left and then been away for a week after that, which was longer than he had ever been away before.

Billy sat there with his arms across his chest and shaking his head the whole time. When I finished, he looked at me. "It sounds like those two scumbags were nicer to you than Eddie was. You should have listened to their advice and left him then. Why didn't you?"

Tears came to my eyes unbidden and surprised me. My hands on the steering wheel gave a shake, and I must have pressed down on the gas unconsciously because the car lurched forward. Taking a deep breath, I began. "You've heard stories of women who are abused and then one day up and kill their husbands? And everyone says, 'Why didn't she just leave?' I'm here to tell you they *can't* leave. Because the men make them feel powerless—

powerless to do anything. *I* couldn't leave. Eddie told me I was fat and ugly and stupid and no one else would ever want me. He made me feel so bad about myself, how could I ever get the courage to leave? He made it out that I was garbage and without him, I'd have nothing. Ever."

"And you believed him?"

I would've glanced at him, but I didn't want him to see my tears, so I tried to drive with my head turned slightly to the left. "Of course I believed him. If someone tells you that day after day after day, you begin to think they're telling you the truth, and when it keeps continuing year in and year out, then you *know* it's the truth. I had no self-esteem and thought I was lucky to have Eddie who still claimed to love me.

"Yes, he did all those terrible things to me, always had at *least* one girlfriend on the side, and all the rest, but he always came back to *me*. In that way, I thought he was rather loyal. And it made me feel loved. So when he told those thugs to kill me, that he'd rather have the money, I *knew* he didn't mean it and that he would return to me, eventually. And I had to believe it because I had no other choice."

"And yet, you did finally leave." Billy looked at me, but I didn't look at him.

"Yes, finally. I got lucky. I'm sure you heard about the Grand Canyon trip and the mules? It's probably all over town by now. I didn't want to go on that trip. It sounded scary. But when we got there and had to get on the mules, Eddie was afraid. I had ridden horses before, so I was the brave one. And I made it down that steep canyon. For some reason, it gave me courage. It gave me confidence. And so, when he said my butt was bigger

152

than the mule's, I reacted from a place of confidence, instead of from fear. Really, I got lucky. If it had happened any other way, I probably wouldn't have left." I pulled into my driveway and turned off the key.

Billy opened his door but didn't step out. Instead, he turned to me, put his hand on my shoulder again and in a soft voice said, "You know I would never do those things to you, Lorry." Carrying Aiden's boots and the dream catcher, he got out of the car and shut the door, leaving me more flabbergasted than ever.

CHAPTER THIRTY-THREE

I SAT THERE in my new car, with the leather seats, the fancy dashboard, the car phone attachment, and I watched Billy walk into my house, all the while wondering what on earth he could have meant by that. It disturbed me so much that I sat there for a few minutes trying to feel normal again. Finally, I opened the door, stepped out, and walked into the house.

Petra was in the living room reading. She looked up when I walked in. "Did you know that it's theorized that the term babysitter may come from hens sitting on their eggs?"

Without answering, I shook my head. "Where's Billy?" Petra didn't require an answer anyway when she told me those things, did she?

"Billy's in the bedroom with Aiden, tucking him in." When I reached into my purse to pay her for babysitting, she shook her head. "Billy already paid me, and he'll take me home in a minute."

I wasn't sure how I felt about that. Aiden was *my* son and *my* responsibility. But I *was* helping Billy out by identifying the two hoods. Although I was also doing it for myself, because the sooner we found another suspect, the sooner the heat would be off me. But Billy had already paid for Petra and Mason's dinner. Where was Mason anyway? Looking around the room, I didn't see him anywhere, but I remembered seeing his motorcycle out front. And why wasn't *he* taking Petra home? It didn't matter. My head felt too confused at that moment to comprehend much of anything, so I walked into my bedroom, closed the door, undressed, and put my robe on. I needed to get into bed and contemplate all that had gone on today.

As I came out of the bedroom, Billy came out of Aiden's room. "He's ready for bed. He wants to see you."

I shrugged and walked in. Aiden was smiling, which made me smile. His smile was enough to light up a whole room. Bingo sat beside him and thumped his tail when he saw me. Sitting down next to Aiden on the bed, I ruffled his hair. "Did you have fun with Petra and Mason?"

"Yeah! We had pizza and played games. And then Sheriff Billy came in and told me about his talk at my school today. They won't bother me anymore, and if they do, he said I'm to tell a teacher right away. When I told him I didn't want to be a tattletale, he said it was my job to straighten out bullies so they wouldn't make anyone else feel bad. That made sense to me, so I told him I would."

I had to stifle a laugh. Billy missed his calling. He should have been a politician. "I'm glad he made you feel better, sweetie."

"And look!" Aiden reached over and pulled the box of boots from the other side of Bingo. I hadn't even noticed them there. "Sheriff Billy bought me boots! Just like his!"

155

He took the boots out of the box and hugged them. "I'm going to sleep with them tonight."

"Okay, but not under the covers, okay?"

"Okay. Mommy, is it okay if we don't read tonight? I'm tired."

I kissed him on his forehead. "Sure, sweetie. We'll catch up tomorrow night." Reaching over to turn out the light beside his bed, I kissed him again, and started to leave the room.

"Oh! Mommy!"

I looked back and in the light from the hallway, I could see that he was holding something up. "What is it, sweetie?"

"Billy asked me to give you this."

When I walked over to his bed, he handed me a five dollar bill. "Hmmmm," I said when I took it from him.

"I told Billy how happy I was that you guys had gotten me a real one with real rawhide instead of one of those fake ones."

"And what did Billy say to that?"

"That's when he reached into his pocket and gave me this. He said you were right." Aiden pointed above his head where his new dream catcher hung on the wall. How did Billy do that so quickly? I hadn't even heard any hammering.

Smiling, I kissed Aiden goodnight again, stashed the bill in my robe pocket, and closed the door halfway to keep the hall light out of his eyes. Petra and Billy had left, and I didn't know where Mason was, but he must have left, too. Maybe a friend of his picked him up, and that's why his motorcycle was still out front. I sank down on the couch and closed my eyes.

After a few minutes of sitting there peacefully, I

planned to go to my bedroom and go to sleep. First, though, I had to unwind. It felt good relaxing in my own home. My mind wandered back to what Billy had said, but before I had a chance to interpret it, I heard footsteps that sounded awfully big to be Bingo's or Aiden's. Opening my eyes, I saw Mason striding toward me.

He was tall and thin with dark eyes and a dirty blond ponytail. His hair wasn't dirty, you understand, that was his hair color, which made me wonder why they would call it dirty. Whatever. The color was somewhere between blond and brown and looked good with his eyes. And he wore what I always saw him in: blue jeans with a light blue work shirt and a denim vest with Greek letters on it. I found out what those Greek letters stood for—Phi Delta Epsilon, the medical fraternity he was in. Mason, who appeared to be a tattooed-up biker, was going to be a doctor. He was one of my first lessons in the pitfalls of assuming and judging.

"Lorry! What are you doing? We're going to play! I have the board all set up in the kitchen. You can have white—I know you need the advantage." He chuckled. Mason and I had played many games of chess over the summer. At first, when I hadn't played in a decade, he won. Then we had a few draws, but ever since I got back into my groove, he hadn't won. But he was good-natured about it and kept trying to beat me.

"Mason, not tonight. I'm tired. I need to get some sleep." It occurred to me that I sounded like his girlfriend declining an evening of romance. Luckily, he didn't see the similarity. Or if he did, he didn't let on. Mason was Petra's boyfriend. I didn't know if they were *doing it* or not. I didn't want to know. It wasn't something I wanted to think about. On the other hand, *thinking* about doing it was as close to *doing it* as I got these days.

Mason stood in front of me, grabbed both of my hands, and tried to pull me up off the couch. Tried being the salient word. "Come on, Lorry. Just one quick game. Please?"

"Mason, *you* come on. It's *chess*. There's no such thing as a *quick* game. Honestly, I just want to go to sleep. It's been a trying day."

He let go of my hands and sat down beside me. "I'm sorry, Lorry. I'm sorry they think you killed that jerk of an ex-husband of yours. I know you well enough to know that if you had killed him, you wouldn't have done it in your own car."

"Thanks, Mason. I appreciate your confidence. I think."

Mason stood up and tugged on my hands again. "Come on, Lorry. It will make you forget your troubles."

"Oh, Mason," I said, knowing as I said it that I was giving in. So I let him pull me to my feet, and I followed him into the kitchen.

Sitting in front of the white, I reluctantly moved one of my pieces forward. The chess set was my *every day* set. My Winnie the Pooh chess set that I had received when I was a child, was in the closet. And my grandiose chess set that had everything except gold plating, was gone for good. I had discovered the pawn receipt in Eddie's pants pocket right next to a match book with *Cheryl* and a phone number written in Eddie's almost illegible script. I rushed over to the pawn shop to get it, but the clerk said they had already sold it. Eddie had pawned it for five hundred dollars, and it was worth thousands.

It was my college graduation gift from my mother. She

hadn't realized that Eddie had convinced me how stupid it was to play chess and had made me quit years before I graduated. Had she known, she would have said it was because Eddie was too stupid to learn to play chess himself. And she would have been right.

The set in front of me was a splendid one: it was the Greek Mythology variety with gods and goddesses as the playing pieces. My favorite piece was the knight depicted as a centaur. For some reason that appealed to me. Mason moved and I moved and Mason moved and I moved. My mind was not on the game. It was on Billy's words to me before he had gotten out of the car. What was that about, anyway? I wasn't paying attention to the game—just moving by rote—when Mason took one of my pawns that I hadn't expected.

"Hey!" When I looked at Mason he had a huge grin on his face.

"En passant, baby! I gotcha!"

"Wait a minute." Quickly, I thought back to my previous move, which wasn't easy because all that would come into my head was Billy's eyes when he said those words, but finally I managed to squeak out the answer. Yes, Mason had played it correctly. "How long have you been holding that one back?" It was a rare move, but legal, and was occasionally used in tournaments. I couldn't fault him.

He straightened up proudly. "I learned it this week."

Shaking my head, I took my move, but something was bothering me. What Billy had said and why he said it and what he meant by it was taking a back seat to something else—but I didn't know what that was. Mason's move had triggered something in me, but I couldn't make out what. The rest of the game was a blur, and I became so unfocused on it that Mason won. He was so excited because it was the first game he had won in months, that he held both arms straight up in a football touchdown celebration, which made me smile.

And then I got excited, because I figured out what it was that bothered me. Mason's unexpected move. Completely unexpected. And I had it. I knew who had killed Eddie.

CHAPTER THIRTY-FOUR

THE DAY BEGAN like any other day, except that Bingo wouldn't stop barking while he was in the backyard. But all the other neighborhood dogs were barking, too, so I didn't think too much about it. Aiden and I ate breakfast, got dressed—Aiden with his new boots on—and started out the front door as usual with Bingo in tow. When I closed the front door, I immediately looked behind us to make sure no one had painted on the door again. So it surprised me when Aiden tugged on my arm and said, "Mommy. Mommy." Bingo barked.

Following Aiden's gaze, I looked in that direction. A new flock of reporters swarmed all over the street—just when I thought it was safe to leave the house. Kasey must have opened her big mouth just as I thought she would. I couldn't wait to get to the office and see what the newspapers had printed.

The reporters must have known better than to set foot on my property, because they stayed on the perimeter. I put Aiden and Bingo in the back seat of the car and as I walked around to the driver's side, the reporters who were not so cautious about the neighbor's yard accosted me before I had a chance to slip into the car.

"Is it true that you inherited millions? Is that why you killed Eddie Keeley? Have you not been arrested because you're involved with the sheriff? Do you think you'll get away with murder?"

The questions didn't stop until I slammed the door on someone's microphone and it fell to the pavement with a thud. But the reporters kept knocking on the windows trying to get questions in until the neighbors turned on their sprinklers driving the vultures off. I waved to the Clarks, who stood on their porch with unidentifiable looks on their faces. They had welcomed me and Aiden into the neighborhood when we first moved in, but we had done little socializing since then. Did they think I did it, too, I wondered. Shaking my head with lament, I started the car and backed out of the driveway.

Making our way down the street was another matter. It was packed with reporters and their cars. We made it to Bridge Street without having to whack one of them, and Aiden rolled down his window to say hello to Martha and Hugo. "Grammy! Grampy!" He waved and they waved back. Then Martha motioned us to the side of the road, so I pulled over.

While Hugo stuck his head into the back seat to ruffle Aiden's hair and pet Bingo, Martha leaned in the front. "Lorry, we haven't seen you in ages. And I know you're under a lot of stress with everything that's going on. Why don't you come for dinner tonight? What do you think? Will you come?"

"Yes, Mommy! Yes! Say yes!" Aiden insisted from the back seat.

"Sure, Martha, if you don't mind the trouble." I motioned to the reporters surrounding the car.

162

"No, I'll invite Billy, too. That will keep them away."

And her making that comment brought something back to me that I had overlooked before. It must have registered on my face because Martha reached her arm through the window to pat my hand.

"Are you okay, dear? If you'd rather it be another time, that's fine."

"No, Martha, everything is fine. Yes, we'll be there. But we need to leave for work now."

Then Hugo piped up from the back window, "Our friendship is real, so we will reveal, how we care, so we'll see you there!" He was always doing that, and I missed his silly poetry.

Aiden laughed, and Hugo and Martha stepped away from the window, and after the goodbyes, I drove off. What Martha reminded me of was what one of the reporters had asked me: "Have you not been arrested because you're involved with the sheriff?" Where did they get that idea? Unfortunately, I knew where they got that idea. Billy and I had gone to the casino together last night, and someone had seen it.

"Aiden, I'm saying this once, and I don't want you to argue." I turned the rearview mirror so I could look at him. "I know how you like for us to walk to school together, but today I'm going to drop you off."

"But—"

"No buts, Aiden. I'm dropping you off." I turned down the street to the school, and as I had feared, the reporters had congregated there. Daniel, the fix-it person in the school, was trying to shoo them away, but there were too many. Luckily, or perhaps by design, Pamela was standing out by the curb and came up to the car when I pulled up.

"Hi, Lorry. Let me take Aiden in. This is terrible! I'll be glad when you're cleared and they find the real culprit!" She opened the back door, and Aiden slipped out and put his arms around her. "Come on, Aiden. I'll protect you from these vultures! Bye, Lorry." She closed the door and, with her arms around Aiden, walked him into the school.

It was a trying situation, and I hated to see Aiden cowed like that, but I smiled. She believed me. Pamela Reilly, principal of Aiden's school, believed me. That meant a lot. At least someone besides Bryan believed me. I thought Billy finally did, but I still wasn't sure about him. He was difficult to read sometimes, and since this whole thing began, he was almost impossible to read. But having one reputable person believe in me meant so much that I didn't know what to do with it. The feeling, I mean. The feeling of being vindicated.

CHAPTER THIRTY-FIVE

WHEN I PULLED into the alley and drove toward the back of the historical society, the reporters' cars were lined up all the way to the street. There were three spots behind the historical society and two behind the Rutledge Koffee Korner Kafe, and all of them filled with reporters. I pulled up behind the cars on the society side and laid on the horn hoping they'd get the idea and move. They didn't, so I pulled out my cell phone to pretend to dial 911.

But I didn't have to pretend, because just then, Billy drove up with his siren on and his lights a-blazing. When I started to move my car, he pulled up beside me. Then he pulled out his ticket book and began writing tickets to the cars parked illegally—at least the ones trapped in front of me that couldn't get away. The ones behind the Koffee Korner drove away without Billy trying to stop them. But the part that bothered me was when I saw some of the reporters take pictures of Billy writing the tickets.

After he finished, he motioned for me to move the car, and he moved his. The reporters moved their cars, and I pulled into my usual spot. Billy stepped out of his patrol car with something in his hands. He walked over to my car and handed me a newspaper.

"It's not good, Lorry. I'll tell you that." He shook his head. "But I'm having a meeting today with Bryan and the private investigator who's been following you. So this will all be over soon."

"Billy, it won't be over until you catch the real murderer."

He backed away and nodded. "You're probably right." Then he walked toward his patrol car, with the reporters still snapping pictures, and he drove away.

After inviting Bingo into the front seat, I opened my door. Quickly, I jumped out of the car with Bingo in my arms, unlocked the back door to the building, and retreated to the relative safety within. Not until I reached my desk did I open the newspaper. There was a big picture of Billy and me in my car with his hand on my shoulder. Although I didn't know where they took the picture, I knew that he had done that a few times during the evening, but only for a few seconds each time. The photographer got lucky. And Billy and I got unlucky. Especially me.

"Aren't you even going to say hello?" called Petra from her office.

I had passed her by without saying a word. "Sorry, Petra. Have you seen this frickin' newspaper?"

"Yes, I saw it. You have to ignore it."

It was only then I realized Petra had not unlocked the front door and reporters were out there pounding on the glass impatient to get in. "We're going to stay closed again today?"

"I think we should." She stood leaning against the wall

between her office and mine.

Then I noticed she had also taken my phone off the hook. "That again?" I pointed to the phone, and she nodded.

"Yeah, I think we should chill today." She looked around. "Aiden in school?"

"Yup. The reporters were there swarming like bees, but luckily Pamela met me at the curb and walked him in herself. Man, I'll be glad when this is over."

"So I see that you didn't duct tape Kasey's mouth shut." Petra turned, stepped to her desk, and stepped back into the room. She plopped a package of duct tape on my desk. "See! I was right! It's Duck Tape!"

I picked it up and looked at it, and it had a stylized picture of a duck on it. "Yes, Petra, but see here. *Duck* is the brand name. Right here it says *duct tape*."

Petra laughed. It was a good laugh, reminiscent of the child in her which was rapidly fading away into womanhood. "I know! I saw that. I just thought it was funny."

The large five-by-five picture dominated the front page of the newspaper, but now I opened it again to look at the headlines. When I saw it, I groaned. "Oh, no, how could it get any worse?" The headline read: *Former Heiress Now an Heiress Again After Allegedly Killing Ex-husband.* I scanned the article, and it had everything that it said in the letter, plus a few embellishments. Groaning again, I closed the newspaper and looked up at the window where the reporters were snapping pictures through the glass. "Isn't there any way we can close this thing so they can't stare at me?"

The window had a sheer panel that was only a few inches wide. Even if I released both sides, instead of

167

having them pulled back, the center part of the window would still be wide open. And from strictly a photographic angle, it would probably provide a good frame.

"Yeah! Just a minute!" And I heard Petra's steps moving toward the exhibit area.

She returned carrying a large sign that she set in the window. It fit perfectly. Now I could look at the vintage sign for Grizelda's Bar. Although it didn't reach the top of the tall window, if the photographers wanted to take a picture of the top of my head, they were welcome to it. I touched the top of my head to make sure there were no stray cowlicks sticking up that might embarrass me—like I was not embarrassed enough already being accused of murder. The whole thing was funny in an unfunny way.

"Is it okay if we borrow this from the exhibit?"

"Sure! Who's going to complain? We're closed today. Remember?"

"Yeah, right. Right. I didn't think about that."

I turned on the computer, but felt too anxious about the whole situation to get anything done. Some of the reporters were pressing their noses against the door glass trying to look in. Finally, I took a deep breath, turned my chair around and gazed at the large fish tank before me. In the tank were Black Moors, black and orange Oranda goldfish, and some Calico Fantails. The Fantails were my favorite. And watching all of them together, swimming casually around, enjoying being alive, reminded me that the world really is a beautiful place. And if you can get past the few bad people and the few bad things that can happen, then you can enjoy life just like those fish.

I don't know how much time I spent gazing at those fish, but just when I was thinking about how pleasant it would feel to be a fish in a fish tank—to know what was coming, to have a neat and orderly life, to know your boundaries—I heard a familiar voice outside my window. So I turned my chair around and stood up so I could see above the sign. There stood Billy, in all his handsome glory, shouting to the reporters. "Repeat! I will do a press conference right here at three o'clock!" He repeated it several more times looking in all directions to make sure everyone heard him. Then, without even looking in the building and acknowledging me, he turned on his heel, walked to his patrol car, and drove off.

CHAPTER THIRTY-SIX

"DID YOU HEAR that, Petra?"

"Hear what? I'm studying."

"Billy outside announcing that he's doing a press conference at three o'clock."

"That should be interesting."

"Yeah, he must have had a good meeting with Bryan and the private investigator."

"What private investigator?"

"You know, the one who has been following me around and taking video of me all this time."

"Oh yeah," said Petra, "that's right."

Then I heard half a jingle sound at the door. It was the boy courier Martha sent over when she had typing for me to do. He tried the door, found it locked, and put the folder of typing into the mail slot. I waved to him and smiled, even though the folder opened and the contents spread across the floor. It wasn't his fault, and I wasn't going to blame him for the rotten circumstances. But it was a hefty lot of papers, and I was grateful for something to do until Billy's press conference, so I wouldn't have to keep thinking about it.

After picking up all the papers, I sat down at my desk, organized said papers, and turned to the computer. When I checked my email, there were a couple of forwards from Petra, and a gloating email from Mason talking about how he had kicked my butt at chess the previous night. It made me laugh. Then, suddenly, I realized that it was at the chess game I had figured out the murder. Setting aside the typing, I immediately opened the top desk drawer where I had hidden the attorneys' letter.

I pulled it out of the envelope and read it again. It was the first line: *It has come to our attention that the threat of you returning to your former husband, Edward Keeley, has been negated.* Jumping up, I hurried to Petra's desk.

"Petra! Listen to this," and I read it aloud to her.

"Yeah, so?"

"Listen again." I repeated just the end of it. ". . . *has been negated.* Tell me that doesn't sound like *they* negated him."

"They who?"

"The attorneys! My mother must have paid them to kill Eddie!"

"Oh, Lorry! Get real. Attorneys don't do that kind of thing."

I sat down in the chair by her desk and looked into her eyes. "Petra, I know that most attorneys don't do that kind of thing. But my mother had mucho bucks. She was incredibly wealthy. She could have put in her will—as a codicil or something—that Eddie was to be *neutralized.* You know, killed. Not only could she afford it, but she was persuasive enough to convince others to do her bidding. I know this is it, Petra! It makes perfect sense."

"Oh, Lorry. You read too many novels." Petra turned

back to her studies.

I stood up. "Petra, don't think too harshly of her. You know all the crap that Eddie did to me. She was only protecting her young—you know, like mother bears do. You can't blame her. At least I don't." Petra continued studying and ignored me, so I walked back to my desk. I sat there, holding the letter in my hands and reading it over and over again. *Negated.* It would only be more clear if they had said *neutralized.* But how would I find out something like that? How could I prove it? Hitmen don't get to be successful hitmen without knowing how to cover their tracks. There was only one place to start. I had to talk to Bryan.

Carefully, as if it was crucial evidence, I folded the letter, put it back into the envelope, and placed it into the drawer. I picked up the phone to make the call, but I had forgotten why it was off the hook. When I pressed down the receiver button, it immediately rang. "Good morning! Rutledge Historical Society!" Someone started asking questions that had nothing to do with the historical society, so without a word I pressed down the button briefly and left it off the hook. Then I reached into my purse and pulled out my cell phone so I could call Bryan. Wait. I didn't have Bryan's telephone number. He had always appeared when I needed him just like my fairy godmother, beginning when I was in the holding cell. Wait, yes I did! I pawed through my purse again searching for the card he gave me that first day. Rolling around at the bottom of my purse, alongside a nail clippers, and the used chewing gum in a wrapper I had taken away from Aiden, was the card. *Bryan O'Keefe Attorney at Law Flagstaff, Arizona.*

When I called the number, it rang and rang. Finally,

the voicemail message popped up. *You have reached Bryan O'Keefe Attorney at Law.* I already knew that. After I heard the beep, I left him a message to call me as soon as he could. I didn't know if he was still in town or if he had returned to Flag.

Returning to the file folder full of papers, I opened a file in Word, and began typing. Hours later, someone pounded on the door. At first I ignored it, not wanting to deal with the reporters. But when the person persisted, I went to the door and saw a couple of families standing out there with pleading looks on their faces.

"Please can we come in? We came all the way from the valley," they said through the glass. They must mean Phoenix because Verde Valley wasn't that far.

I opened the door, and they started explaining the trip and how they came just to see the Rutledge Historical Society, but I nodded and pointed them down the hallway. "The exhibits begin right there. Hope they don't disappoint you." There wasn't much to the exhibits, so I wanted them to know beforehand.

The two sets of parents and five assorted children smiled and happily followed my finger down the hallway. I left the front door unlocked, and it wasn't long before a couple of reporters stuck in their heads. But I shooed them out and locked the door behind them.

My cell rang, and it was Bryan. He was quiet while I explained my thoughts. When I finished, he said, "It sounds a little outrageous, but not completely unheard of. I'll investigate!" And that was a lot more credence than I thought he'd give me for such a crazy idea. I believed it, yes, but I also thought it was crazy. Bryan clicked off, and I returned to the typing.

After the families were back in the exhibit area for an

hour, I wondered if they were loading the stuff up in their pockets, but then I remembered that it was all locked up. And I could hear their voices, both the adults and the children. So it wasn't as if they were sneaking around back there or anything. Sometime later, they all came out and piled into the gift shop. It was small and could barely accommodate both families. Fifteen minutes later, they piled out again, their arms full of t-shirts, sweatshirts, posters, postcards, and one kid held an ashtray that must have been in that gift shop from the dark ages. Did people still use those things anymore?

Petra took their money, and I stood up to unlock the door and let them out. One kid pointed to the sign in front of my window and said, "There it is! That's the sign that's missing."

I shrugged my shoulders guiltily. "Sorry. I had to borrow it."

As they walked out they whispered among themselves probably saying how exciting it was to be in the same building as someone who had committed mariticide. Except that was killing your husband. What would killing your ex-husband be—not that I did kill him, mind you—but I wondered if it would be ex-mariticide or marit-ex-icide or what? That's probably a question that will go unanswered for eternity.

CHAPTER THIRTY-SEVEN

IN THE MIDST of typing one of the last documents, I heard something outside and stood up to look out the window over the sign that was still there. The two young deputies were setting up three pallets in front of the historical society's door. Sitting back down, I rolled my chair to the left in front of the door to get a better view. When they got the pallets aligned just so, they set up a large speaker on either side. A mob of reporters milled around trying to attain the most desirable position close to the front. There were two trucks parked on the other side of the street from local television stations. This was the biggest deal in Rutledge since Wyatt Earp and Doc Holiday had stopped here on their way to Prescott. *If* they really did, that is.

One of the deputies, I think it was the one named Derek, tried the handle, and when he found it locked, he knocked on the door as he held up an electrical cord. Opening the door, I pointed under the desk, where I thought the only plug was. He crawled under there, plugged it in, and left without even saying thank you. Don't parents teach their children anything anymore? A child that never says thank you turns into an adult that never says thank you. Shameful! I thought. Absolutely shameful! Then I had to laugh at myself. My getting over being judgmental wasn't going very well! At least I recognize it. That's moving in the right direction, isn't it?

At a few minutes before three, I heard the back door of the society open and heavy footsteps stride quickly down the aisle. I didn't even have to turn around to know who it was. I heard Petra say, "Hi, Billy," as he passed, but he only mumbled in return. When I said hello, he gave me the same response without looking my way. He unlocked and opened the door and stepped out, closing the door behind him.

In my life, I have found that when men had something on their minds, they were focused on just that thing, and nothing else could penetrate their consciousness until the first thing was concluded. And Billy was, after all, a man, so I wasn't going to take offense at his brusqueness. Besides, he had done the same thing to Petra, and they had been close friends for years.

Billy stepped onto the arranged pallets, took the microphone from one of the deputies, and began talking. With the microphone on and the speakers so close, I could hear every word he said.

"My name is Billy Madrigal, and I am the Sheriff of Rutledge County. The woman inside this building, Lorry Lockharte, has gained *undeserved* notoriety for having her ex-husband found dead in her car." I could hear some reporters in the crowd say something, but their voices didn't carry inside. Billy raised his arms and brought them down, indicating the crowd to quiet. "Yes, I understand that she is also the one who found the body. But as you all must realize, this is purely circumstantial evidence."

He reached behind him and pulled some papers out of his pocket. "I have here a sworn testimony from a third party about her whereabouts on the morning that Edward Keeley was found dead." Here he began reading from the papers, the same papers that Bryan had when I was in the holding cell, starting with "Eight A.M. let the dog out," to "9:05, arrive back at the historical society and found body." But I heard the reporters' voices rise again, and Billy's arms stretched out to quiet them down again.

"In addition, when she arrived at the historical society at 8:47, *she had her son in the car with her!*" He spoke those words louder and slower than the rest, and then continued. "There was no dead body in the front seat then! When she was at school, she talked to the principal, Mrs. Pamela Reilly, and was seen by probably a hundred people. She could not have killed Edward Keeley and been at the school at the same time." Voices rose again, and Billy quieted them down once again. One of the deputies—the other one, named Nick—handed him something. It looked like a CD. Billy held it up.

"In my hand, I have a video of Lorry Lockharte's morning. In it, you can see everything she did on the morning of the murder. You can see the empty car seat when she set off to walk her son to school, and you can see her finding the body when she returned to the car. This video—"

Aiden ran down the hallway and burst into the room. "What's going on, Mom? Why is Sheriff Billy outside speaking to the reporters?" He put his hand on the doorknob to open it, when I stopped him.

"Aiden, come here." I hugged him. "You can't go out

177

there. Billy needs to finish what he's doing."

"What's he doing, though?" Aiden squirmed out of my arms and stood in front of the door, but he didn't touch the knob again.

"He's explaining to the reporters why your mommy couldn't have committed the murder."

Aiden put his hands on his hips and looked at me. "Finally! It's about time he stood up for you!"

I stifled a laugh, reached over and pulled the Grizelda sign from the window. "Can you do Mommy a favor and return this to the exhibit? I don't think I'll be needing it anymore."

"Sure, Mom." He took the sign out of my hands—it was almost as big as he was—and carried it to the back.

Billy opened the door, turned the sign to *Open*, and looked at me. "You can stay open now. I think that will take care of the reporters for you, Lorry. If you have any other trouble with them, let me know." Then he walked toward the back, but Aiden must have met him in the hallway, because I heard him scream with delight, which is what happens when Billy swings him around.

Looking out the window, I saw the two deputies, Nick and Derek, handing out the CDs to the reporters. When the street had cleared, they began dismantling the makeshift stage.

I pulled the plug on the electrical cord, opened the door, and tossed it out. There was a woman standing outside the window who looked vaguely familiar, but I couldn't place her. Then I saw Renee Croft and her sister Rita, both of them looking stern, march past the deputies and pull the door open. I braced myself, but stayed seated. Sometimes appearing smaller is better than inviting confrontation. And it's not often that I can appear smaller, so I figured I'd take advantage of it.

Once inside, Renee gave Rita a shove toward me. I could see by her tear-stained face that she had been crying. So I did the polite thing; I said, "I'm sorry for your loss, Rita."

Renee jerked her sister back, but not before I noticed something about Rita's finger. Renee stepped forward and leaned down so her face was an inch from mine. Bingo, hiding behind my chair, was barking furiously at her. "You're sorry?" Renee screamed. "You're sorry that you killed my sister's boyfriend—when *you're* the one who did it?" Slowly, she stood up straight and raised her arm to slap me across the face, but I didn't move.

Billy, without Renee noticing, had come up behind her. He grabbed her by the wrist and pulled her around so she was facing him. Then he dropped her wrist. With his face angrier than I had ever seen him, he said quietly, "You're welcome, Ma'am."

Renee, who was never the brightest bulb in the pack, stood up to her full height—not as tall as Billy, but with her athletic body, she still appeared formidable—looked him in the eye, and said, "Why should I thank *you?*"

"For saving you an assault charge. Now get out of here and leave this woman alone!" When she stood there looking at him for a beat longer than Billy thought she should, Billy added, "I mean now! Git!" Renee opened the door and dragged Rita outside with her.

Without saying another word, Billy returned to the back, and I heard Aiden scream with delight again. And everything returned to normal. Out my window, I could see Renee walk by and look in. She mouthed "I'll get you for this!" as she pushed into the familiar-looking woman who was looking more familiar by the second.

Before I had a chance to process Renee's vitriol, my cell phone rang. It was Bryan, who began speaking before I even said hello. The door opened, and as much as I hated to, I told him I'd have to call back. Before I looked up to see who had entered, I had to get my bearings. Because Bryan had just told me that the attorneys had killed Eddie, just as I thought.

CHAPTER THIRTY-EIGHT

THE PERSON WHO stepped inside was the familiar looking woman from outside. It took me a second and a half to recognize her. I jumped up and threw my arms around her. "Sam! I can't believe it's you! Sam!" Stepping back, I looked at her for an instant and then hugged her again.

"Lorry, so good to see you." Samantha Kohn, formerly Samantha Katz, was my best friend in high school. But she moved back east to go to college, and I hadn't seen her since. She got involved with and married Mark Kohn, and I got involved with and married Eddie. And then Eddie put a stop to our friendship. Eddie put a stop to everything that I loved. Sam lived on my block, back in the old days, and was one of the rich kids, so we had that in common. Today, she looked casual with beige slacks and a beige striped blouse, but the clothing looked expensive. Some things never change. Sam and I had always both been clothes hounds.

"How did you know I was back here again?" Last time I had written her—which was years before—Eddie and I had been living in Coyote Moon.

"Oh, you know, the town gossip." She used her thumb to indicate the Rutledge ˙ Koffee Korner Kafe. "Your cousin, you know. I could never remember her name because you called her something different. I can't remember what it was, but it had to do with Dalmatians!"

"Cruella DeVille! The evil woman who stole the hundred and one Dalmatians!"

"That's right. And you called her that because she took your first grade boyfriend," she hesitated and put up her palm to stop me from saying anything. "Don't tell me. Oh, yeah! Conrad Hayes!"

"What a memory you have! It's so good to see you, Sam. So I suppose the town gossip also told you that Eddie was dead?"

"Yes, and that you had previously filed for divorce. And then I heard the sheriff talking to the reporters. They really thought you did it?"

I shrugged. "Well, I not only had a lot of good reasons to, but the jerk was found in my car!"

"Oh. Not good. But it sounds like the sheriff has gotten you off the hook."

"For now, but he better find out who *really* did it pretty quick, or the sharks will probably start another feeding frenzy with me being the feed!"

"I hope he finds him fast then. For your sake."

"So what are you doing in town? I didn't think you'd ever come back here. Your folks left, right?"

Sam laughed. "I didn't think *you* would ever return here, either! Yeah, my folks left right after I graduated high school. My dad got a better paying job in Kansas City."

"So what are you doing here?"

182

"Well, how ironic is this? Mark's parents decided to retire in Phoenix. They've been there for a year. So now Mark feels like he should be in Arizona so they can continue their relationship with our kids."

"I didn't know you had children."

"I sent you letters, I sent you pictures. And I sent a Christmas and birthday card every year until they started coming back labeled 'Not at this address. Return to sender.'"

Shaking my head, I clenched my fist and whispered, "I swear, if he wasn't already dead, I *would* kill him!"

"So you didn't get any of those letters, then? I wondered why you never answered, but I figured you were busy."

"No, I never got a single one. You weren't even pregnant when I thought you had stopped writing. Eddie kept a close eye on me. I can't believe I stayed with him as long as I did." Starting to get angry at him all over again, I made myself shake it off.

"Here, let me show you a picture of the kids." She reached into her shoulder bag and pulled out her wallet. She flipped through and proudly held up a picture of a cute little boy and girl. The boy was Aiden's age, about seven, and the girl looked about three or four.

"Oh, they're beautiful! What are their names?"

Sam smiled at the picture. I could see how much she loved her children. "That's Sage, and she's Willow."

"They're beautiful, Sam. So you're moving to the valley then?"

Sam had a funny look on her face. "Mark wants to move here."

"That's great!" Then I noticed the look on her face. "Ah, but you don't want to. How come?"

She stepped forward and motioned out the window with her chin. "I heard what went on in here. Did you see what *she* did as she walked by?"

Nodding, I said, "You mean Renee. It looked like she didn't know you were there and accidentally bumped into you."

Sam shook her head vehemently. "Oh, no. She noticed me as she came out the door and deliberately ran right into me. I always thought she was a little meshuga."

"Meshuga?" I asked.

"Oh, sorry, Lorry. I'm going to have to educate you all over again. It means crazy. I always thought Renee was a little crazy."

Sam Kohn was Jewish and liked sprinkling her speech with Yiddish words. Back in high school, I eventually got to know what most of them meant. But there had been a lot of years under my belt since then.

"Mark is leaving the move up to me," Sam continued, "and I was leaning toward moving here. I mean, it's been more than ten years! *She* couldn't hold a grudge that long. But apparently she did." She shook her head again. "Oh, no. That little display convinced me. That was a sign from the universe. We can't move here. Ever. Not with *that* woman still in town."

I sighed. "Well, if it's any consolation, she's totally after *me* right now."

"Yes, and that might be why she ran into me like that. She knows I'm your friend." Shaking her head again, she said, "After all these years, she's still a little nuts, isn't she?"

"I'm not sure if 'nuts' would describe her, but maybe it would," I said as I remembered the events of the past

184

few days. Then I told Sam in detail about the paint on my front door and the phone call. "She's whacked, all right."

"But the sheriff thought the murderer did both of those things, right?"

"I suppose he could be right, but my bets are on crazy Renee."

Sam stepped closer and put her hand on my arm. "Lorry, we never talked about it, but I know all the rumors about what happened to your sister. This must all be a reminder of that."

"Yeah, it is. But I couldn't do anything about it back then, and I can't do anything about what she's doing now."

A sound emanated from Sam's purse. She reached in and pulled out her cell phone. "Hi, darlin'. . . . Sure, I'll be at the historical society. You know where that is? . . . See ya in a few." She looked at me. "That was Mark. He's a good man."

"I'm glad you got lucky, even if I didn't!"

"That sheriff, when he was defending you, I got the feeling—"

"Oh! Everybody says that, and it's not true! We're just friends." I leaned closer. "I might like there to be more, but apparently he doesn't feel the same way. He practically arrested me!"

"Yes, but didn't the body fall out of your car in front of him?"

"Cruella DeVille doesn't leave anything out, does she?"

Sam laughed at that and I joined her. Just as a car pulled up out front, Aiden came running up from the back.

"Mommy!" He jumped into my arms.

"I didn't know you and Eddie had a son!"

Aiden, back on the floor, looked up at Sam. "Who's Eddie?"

"Sam, this is *my* son, Aiden. Aiden, this is my best friend, Sam."

Aiden stuck out his hand. "Nice meeting you, Sam! Any friend of Mom's is a friend of mine!"

Sam laughed and shook his hand. "Nice meeting you, Aiden." The car outside beeped its horn softly. "Bye, Lorry! So great seeing you!" She hugged me and opened the door. "Nice meeting you, Aiden. Lorry, I'll be in touch!"

"Bye, Sam. So great to see you!" The car—it looked like a rental—drove away with my best friend in the whole world inside it.

CHAPTER THIRTY-NINE

SITTING DOWN AT my desk, I pulled Aiden onto my lap. "Where is Sheriff Billy? I thought he was back there with you."

"He left and said to tell you that he'd see us at Grammy and Grampy's house at five-thirty."

"Okay, good." I looked at my watch and saw that I still had more than an hour before we left. Then I heard footsteps coming down the hallway.

"Hi, Bryan." Aiden slid off my lap, walked toward Bryan, and then turned back to me. "Mommy, I'm going to read in Petra's office."

"Okay, sweetie. Thanks." I stood up to talk to Bryan in a soft voice so Aiden wouldn't hear. "Sorry, I had to get off the phone so quick. Someone was coming in. Tell me *every*thing." I shook my head and grimaced. "I *knew* those attorneys killed him," I whispered.

"Well, they didn't, Lorry. You hung up before I had a chance to tell you the whole story. And I wouldn't have gotten any of this but an old roommate from law school works in that office—that roommate is how I got this job."

Quicker than I care to admit, as soon as Bryan mentioned an old roommate, an image of some petite little co-ed popped into my mind. Bryan didn't seem like the type to be attracted to some busty blond like Eddie was. But still, his next sentence surprised me.

"Yeah, he's a partner in the firm. He was in the room with your mom when the instructions for the will were drawn up. The attorneys rejected it, of course. Illegal stipulations are unenforceable, but your mother did put it out there. My friend said there were some strange looks going around the table. But he was certain they never hired the hitman. I don't know how he knew, and I didn't want to ask!"

"I don't blame you, Bryan! 'I can tell you, but now I'll have to kill you!'"

Bryan nodded and looked at the ground. "Yeah, something like that."

"Well, thanks for telling me, Bryan. I appreciate it. I knew I couldn't put anything past my mother. This doesn't surprise me."

"From what I understand, she was a character."

"That doesn't begin to describe her."

"Anyway, I wanted to let you know the whole story before you went ballistic on me. How's the new car?"

"It's wonderful, Bryan, thank you."

"No problem. Glad it's working out for you. I can't get your old one sold until Billy solves the case, which will hopefully be soon."

"Hopefully. Yeah. Exactly. Hopefully. It couldn't happen soon enough for me."

"Well, I'll see you later, Lorry. Bye, now."

"Bye, Bryan."

As he walked away, I heard Aiden in the other room

188

call out, "Bye, Bryan." I turned my chair back to the computer so I could finish typing. Before I had typed even a paragraph, I heard Petra's footsteps behind me, so I turned around to face her. It was interesting, she still wore multiple earrings, her hair was still pink, and she still had all her tattoos, but I didn't see her as a weirdo anymore. I saw her as a friend.

"Hey, Lorry, what did Bryan say about your mother's attorneys? They didn't do it, right?" She looked at me and nodded. "Attorneys don't do that kind of thing." When I didn't respond right away, she continued, "Right? They didn't do it, did they?"

Smiling, I said, "Now you don't sound as sure as you were before. It's not such a crazy idea after all, is it? How come you changed your mind?"

"I heard Bryan in here whispering. If they didn't do it, I didn't think he'd whisper." Petra sat on the edge of my desk. "Come on, Lorry, tell me. Did they or didn't they?"

"Bryan said that my mother did ask them to 'dispose' of Eddie, but the attorneys declined." I explained the details to Petra, and she listened with eyes opened wide.

"Wow, wow, wow, Lorry! You were almost right—you *were* right about her asking them to do it. How'd you know?"

"I know my mom, and I know how much she hated Eddie."

"So now we're back to not having a clue about who killed Eddie."

"No, I just discovered—" I couldn't go on because Aiden, his face shining with that inner light that he had, ran into the room and jumped into my arms.

"I finished the chapter, Mom! Is it time to leave yet?"

Petra reached out and ruffled his hair. "You little

rascal! You know it's not five o'clock!"

He pushed her hand away with a big grin on his face. "Close enough! C'mon, let's go to Grammy and Grampy's house and see Billy!"

"Aiden, you just saw Billy. He barely left."

Aiden jumped off my lap and jumped up and down. "I want to see him again! Billy! Billy! Billy!"

I wanted to be strict and make him stop causing a scene, but he made both Petra and me laugh, so I couldn't. Petra recovered before I did.

She stood up. "It's okay, Lorry. I can handle everything here. You guys can go now."

"Yippee! Yippee! Yippee!" Aiden added, clapping his hands to go along with his jumping up and down.

"I need five minutes to finish the typing, Aiden, then we can go. But you need to calm down before we get to Grammy and Grampy's house."

Immediately, he stopped jumping up and down. He put his hands at his sides, put a sweet little smile on his face, and looked like an angel.

"You really know how to play to the audience, don't you, Aiden?" I turned back to my typing and realized once again how lucky I was to have a kid like Aiden.

CHAPTER FORTY

WE LEFT THE office before five, and since we were early, I wanted to go home and change, but Aiden wanted to go straight there. "Aiden," I said, "let's go home so I can change clothes."

"Mommy, if we go home to change, what shoes will you wear?

"High heels."

"Then why go home and change? You have heels on now!"

Since I couldn't argue with that logic, I drove straight to Martha and Hugo's house. It was early, and that was okay, because then I could talk to them before Billy arrived. I wanted to explain everything that had happened in the last week. I'm sure Rutledge was flying with rumors, and I wanted them to know the whole truth.

Turning onto Meadowside Lane, I pulled up into the driveway of the tall, gray Victorian—next to Billy's truck. He had beaten me there and probably for the same reason—to explain everything to Martha and Hugo—from his point of view. But instead of being inside talking to them, he was standing outside and looking like he hadn't gone in yet.

Billy ambled up to the car and opened the back door. "Hiya, little pard!" He wore tight black jeans and a cowboy shirt, and he looked *good.*

"Hi, Sheriff Billy!" Aiden jumped out of the car and into Billy's arms. Billy swung him around and put him back down. "Sheriff Billy, did I do okay?"

After looking at his watch, Billy picked him up and swung him around again. "You did perfect, little pard, perfect."

I stepped out of the car and looked at the two conspirators standing there trying to look innocent. My gaze fell on Billy. "It was your doing getting him to beg to leave early? Very clever, Billy." Shaking my head, I turned to walk into the house.

Billy gently took my arm. "Lorry, wait." He turned to Aiden. "Little pard, would you go into the house with Grammy and Grampy and ask if you can play in the back? Okay?"

"Sure, Sheriff Billy." He reached up to hug Billy's neck as Billy leaned down, and then he reached up to kiss me. "See ya soon, Mom."

Aiden always made me smile. "Sure, sweetie. See ya soon."

Billy led me by the arm toward his truck. "C'mon over here, Lorry." He deposited me by the tailgate and opened the back door, pulled out an old jacket, pulled out the tailgate and began wiping it down. Rubbing his hand over it and showing me there was no dust or dirt, he said, "That okay, Lorry?"

I looked at him sideways, wondering what was going on, and sat down. "Sure, Billy, what's going on?"

Billy sat next to me and said, "I wanted to talk to you before we went in."

"Good, I wanted to talk to you, too, because I discovered something today that might be relevant to the case."

Although he seemed shy and unsure of himself when he sat down, that comment perked him up. "Really? What? What did you discover?"

"It's Eddie's girlfriend, Rita Croft. She had a ring mark on her finger!"

Billy looked confused. "A *what*?"

I held out my left hand where my wedding ring used to reside. My ring mark had long since disappeared. Pointing to my ring finger on my left hand, I said, "Right here. It's how women can sometimes tell if a man is cheating on his wife. He has taken off his ring, but the white mark is still there from where the ring was. Rita had a white mark like she had recently taken off a wedding ring! I think she and Eddie got married!"

"Married?" He nodded his head and looked into the distance like he was thinking. "But, why would that mean anything?" Before I could answer, he added, "You're not divorced yet, are you?"

"No, it's not final yet—I mean it wasn't final when he died. And to answer your first question, isn't the spouse the main person on the suspect list? And if they were married, then she could have taken out life insurance on him! Motive! That is—motive besides Eddie being a jerk. She probably wouldn't get the money if they aren't actually married, but she can still try, right?"

"Lorry, shhh! You can't say anything bad about Eddie right now. I gave the press conference and all, but there is still doubt in some people's minds." He looked at me, scowled, then gazed into the distance again.

"I know what you're thinking—you already checked her out, and she's in the clear. Right?"

"I, uh, called her aunt."

"That's all? You didn't check out airplane tickets or gas receipts? Nothing?" I pulled away to look at Billy, because I couldn't believe that he was so naive.

Billy sighed deeply and shook his head. "I'm sorry, Lorry. All I did was call the aunt, because at that point, I was still thinking there was a good possibility that you were the one who did it."

"Me? Really? You thought that?"

He kept his head down without looking at me. "I had to."

"What do you mean, you had to?"

Billy sighed again, pushed himself into the bed of the truck, leaned against the side, and stretched out his long legs. When I turned to look at him, he held up his hand. "No, Lorry, I need to sit here to tell you this story— which is what I wanted to talk to you about today, anyway. Turn around and just listen." Then he leaned forward and put his hand on my shoulder. "If that's okay, Lorry. Is it? Okay, I mean?"

His voice sounded so soft and pathetic, what could I say? No, I need to look into your eyes while you confess whatever it is you need to confess to me? Instead of that, matching his softness, I replied, "Yes, Billy, it's fine. Go ahead."

Before Billy began, I heard the staccato of the cicadas from the meadow behind the house. The rise and fall of their sounds, like each one copying the other. It made me shiver. And as if one, they stopped, and there was a second of silence.

That's when Billy began his story. A story so sad that it was all I could do not to weep aloud.

CHAPTER FORTY-ONE

BILLY'S FATHER HAD been a sheriff in western Massachusetts where Billy grew up. While Billy was away at college, there were a string of shoplifting incidents in the town. His Aunt Jane, Billy's mother's older sister, was present at every one of the incidents. Billy's father knew she didn't do it and never questioned her, because her innocence was assumed.

Months dragged on and the incidents increased, and still Aunt Jane was present at every one. Pressure to find the culprit was getting worse. It was a small town with small businesses that had narrow profit margins. Everyone in town—except Billy's mother and her sister, Jane—wondered why Jane hadn't been at least formally questioned.

Then came the election. Billy's father had been the sheriff for so long that nobody ever bothered to run against him. But this time, another man ran against him. Although the man was not well liked in the community because of dirty business dealings, he still garnered forty-five percent of the vote. Billy's father was devastated and didn't know what to do. Aunt Jane was elderly, and he didn't want to upset her. And yet, the whole town was turning against him. What could he do?

When months went by with no resolution to the shoplifting, and Aunt Jane still present at every one, the citizens in town collected signatures for a recall election. Billy said he remembered coming home to visit during school break, and when he saw how bad off his father was, he sat down with him and tried to persuade him to at least question Aunt Jane to appease the town. Billy told his father that at least it would look like he was trying to do something.

But his father had been adamant that Aunt Jane did not do this. And to put her through that to show fake effort to the town was not something he was about to do. Integrity was more important than his standing in the community. But the community's attitude was killing him. And there was nothing Billy could do about it.

Before the recall election occurred, Aunt Jane was hospitalized. And the shoplifting incidents continued. Although Billy's father felt vindicated, the whole affair had taken so much out of him that he put in his resignation before the election even took place. It killed him to quit the job he had loved for so many years, but he said it bothered him more that the people of the community had lost faith in him.

The woman doing the shoplifting, a woman of wealth with a mental condition, was apprehended a short time later, and all the stolen goods found in her possession. But Billy's father took the whole episode so hard that he withered away to nothing and ended up dying of a heart attack before a year was out.

At this point in the story, Billy sighed. I dared a quick glance over my shoulder and spied tears running down

Billy's face, so I turned back around before he noticed me.

He sniffled quietly. "And that's why I took you in right away—and even why I thought you did it. Because all that time that my father was defending poor innocent Aunt Jane, I was secretly thinking that she did it. And after my father died—what I believe to be of a broken heart—I swore that would never happen to me. If the people wanted me to bring someone in, it wouldn't matter who it was, I would do it.

"And now, after all that's happened, I think my father was right. It didn't turn out well for him, but he kept his integrity to the end. Thanks to you, Lorry, I finally understand my father. I never forgave him for being so stubborn about that. But now—yes, now I can forgive him. Because I understand completely. I should have never taken you in, and I'm sorry about that. In my heart," he pointed toward the center of his chest, "I knew you didn't do it."

"Thank you, Billy. I appreciate that. What happened to college?"

"When my father had his heart attack, I quit. And I never returned." He pulled his legs toward him, pivoted, and pushed himself off the tailgate. Wiping his eyes surreptitiously, he grabbed my arm, helped me off the tailgate, and said, "C'mon. Enough talking. Let's go in."

I stopped, because he hadn't answered my question about college, at least not completely. He tried to pull me along, but I held firm. Then Hugo called from the doorway of the house.

"Time for dinner!"

Aiden stepped out beside him and jumped up and down. "Let's eat! I'm hungry!"

Reluctantly, I walked to the house with Billy. He didn't say anything, and neither did I. We walked into the kitchen—the dining room was used for bed and breakfast morning guests—and sat at the table. Platters of roasted chicken, broccoli, and brown rice were already on the table. Each of the five place settings had a green salad beside it. Their eating habits had definitely changed since Hugo had his heart attack. And it showed. Hugo had lost a ton of weight. He wasn't exactly slender yet, but he was definitely heading in that direction.

Hugo and Martha sat down, and Hugo said, "Let's dig in! Aiden, can I give you a piece of chicken?"

"Yes, please, Grampy."

A few minutes went by with us discussing innocent topics like the weather, Martha's job, my job, Hugo's weight loss, and then after thirty seconds of silence, Hugo spoke up again. "All right, we've covered all the innocuous subjects, now let's get to what's really important. Tell us about the murder, Billy!"

Martha said, "Hugo!"

"Oh, come on, Martha, you want to know, too. Admit it!"

Aiden put down his fork and cleared his throat. "Sheriff Billy put my mommy in jail!" He glared at Billy.

"I thought you two were friends again?" I asked.

"Yeah, but this just reminded me of what happened." Aiden looked down and resumed eating.

After Billy's sad story and my understanding of it, I felt bad for the poor guy. But I started from the beginning when I found Eddie's body in my car, continued on to my brief incarceration, Billy's press conference, *murderer* painted on my door, the phone call screaming murderer at me, and where we stood now.

Billy was silent until the end.

"Tomorrow I'm going to San Francisco to check on Rita Croft's alibi."

That was a shocker to me. He hadn't mentioned he was going to do that while we were talking. "You are?"

Billy shrugged. "Makes sense."

Hugo and Martha left the subject alone after that, Aiden resumed smiling, and I was left wondering what, if anything, Billy would find out in San Francisco.

CHAPTER FORTY-TWO

THE FOLLOWING DAY at work was murder—if you'll pardon the expression. I hadn't talked to Billy again, so I had no idea when he planned to go. I called the sheriff's station, and they said he was out of the office. When I feel nervous like that, I clean. So I cleaned the bathroom, washed the cat's dish, dusted the exhibits in the back, carried more books upstairs, dusted up there. I found Bingo and Rocky snuggled up on a rug in the back. It doesn't get much cuter than that.

When I finished the cleaning, I returned to my desk to check my email. Nothing of interest except Mason challenging me to another game of chess. He was still gloating over his last win. I'd fix that. I emailed him back and said, "Name the day, buster! Your winning streak has ended!" Before I could chuckle to myself over that one, he had already emailed me back saying, "Tonight you die, sister!" Wait! That email wasn't from Mason. It was from a Lizzie Borden.

"Lizzie Borden!" I pushed away from the desk so fast that my rolling chair almost went over backward.

"What?" asked Petra from the other room.

"Petra! Come here! Please! Now! Come here." I was on my feet with my face in my hands.

"Jeez, Lorry. What's up? I'm studying!" She stood there with her hands on her hips.

"Look at that email." I pointed to the computer screen. "The one from Lizzie Borden."

"Who's Lizzie Borden?" Petra shrugged. "A friend with a weird sense of humor?"

"Lizzie Borden, Petra! You know. Lizzie Borden the ax murderer from the nineteenth century!"

"I know, but I don't get it. Someone with a sick sense of humor trying to scare you? Forget it!"

"Petra! It's from Eddie's murderer! And it's a woman! I was right!"

"What makes you think it's a woman? It could be a man using Lizzie Borden's name."

"Think about it. There are dozens of male serial killers that a man could have chosen: Ted Bundy, Jeffrey Dahmer, the Boston Strangler, the Zodiac Killer, Richard Speck, and more! There were tons to choose from. But our killer chose the most famous female killer, Lizzie Borden." I moved my head slowly from side to side. "It's a woman, Petra. It is *so* a woman. And I know who the woman is. It's Rita Croft!"

"There were other female killers."

"Yeah, but Lizzie Borden is the most famous. Can you name any other women killers?"

Petra shrugged again and returned to her office. "No. Call Billy, then. You better tell him that you received this. He might be more excited about it than I am."

"That's for sure, Petra! I might as well have showed you a picture of a cute dog!"

"I'm studying, Lorry. And I don't have as much at

stake as you do."

"Someone just threatened my life, Petra!"

"I'm sure it's just a prank email. Or spam. Call Billy."

"I can't call Billy, because he's in San Francisco right now as we speak, checking up on Rita Croft's alibi. And I can't reach him."

"Is that why you've cleaned the toilet twenty times already? You know, Lorry, this is Arizona, and we need to conserve water. Next time, just dust!"

"Some friend you are, Petra." Then my email dinged, and I gasped. "Oh, no! Another one." I tiptoed back to my computer—so no one would hear me coming, I guess —and peeked at the new email.

This one was from Mason. "Order the pizza. Tell Petra, and I'll be there at six."

"What does this one say, Lorry? Something more threatening than the spam?"

"It's not spam. No, this one's from Mason. It—" But I couldn't get any more out because Petra was already pushing me aside to read the email from Mason.

She smiled at me. "Well, Lorry, in case it wasn't spam, how about if Mason and I spend the night at your house to protect you?"

"Fine, but you'll sleep in separate rooms. And I still can't believe you're not taking this seriously after the red paint and the phone call. I think that you don't love me." I crossed my arms across my chest and pouted.

Petra put her hands on my shoulders and kissed the top of my head. "Of course I love you, Lorry. It's just that I'm not afraid of empty threats. My father makes them all the time."

That got me to thinking. Perhaps I was being too hard on Petra not fearing for my life. Her father was the town drunk—one of them, anyway—and if he made empty drunken threats to her, no wonder she was not reacting. You know that saying about walking a mile in someone else's moccasins? Well, here is a good example. In this case, it would be sandals, though. I had to walk a mile in Petra's sandals, so I could understand where she was coming from.

CHAPTER FORTY-THREE

JUST AFTER ONE o'clock in the afternoon, my cell phone rang. It was Billy. My hand was shaking so badly that I could barely hold onto the phone. "Billy! What happened?"

"I'm at the airport getting ready to board. My phone has been going in and out, so I hope I have time to give you the info. But I knew you'd be anxious to hear. I just came from Rita Croft's so-called aunt's house. What I found out was—"

And the phone went dead! I gave him a minute to call me back, and when he didn't, I called him. Again and again. It kept going to voicemail. After fifteen minutes without hearing from him, I figured he had already boarded the plane. I'd have to wait. The only clue I had was that he had said "so-called aunt." That had to mean that she wasn't really Rita's aunt. Maybe there was something to this after all.

Dispensing with the bathroom, I carried more books upstairs, arranged them, dusted them, and dusted anything else I could find. Petra teased me a little, but mostly she ignored me and just studied. I even sat on the floor upstairs with the cat in my lap. There are few things in this world as calming as a purring cat in your lap. I'm a dog person, but I can appreciate a purring cat as much as the next gal. I sneezed and my eyes and throat itched, but it was worth it.

Before Aiden came in from school, I called Kasey to see if she minded if Aiden spent the night. If someone *was* going to try to kill me tonight, I didn't want Aiden around. Kasey said yes, and I told her that I'd drop him off after work.

When Aiden came in, he hugged me, and then sat in Petra's spare chair to read with Bingo at his feet. If I told him, he would be too excited to do anything except nag me about when we were going to leave. The last hours dragged by, and I felt grateful when five o'clock finally arrived. Before I stood up to leave for the day, I made a screen print of the offending email and sent it to my home computer.

"Hey, Lorry? Can I have a ride to your house?"

"Petra's coming over?" I heard Aiden say.

"Shhh, Aiden," said Petra.

I didn't want to bring her over this early, because I was hoping for some alone time before Mason arrived at six. But I knew that would be downright rude to tell Petra that I didn't want her to come over this early. Yes, I could be rude at times, but downright rude was further than I really wanted to go. "Yes, Petra, of course. And yes, Aiden, Petra is coming over, but you're not going home tonight."

"What, why not?" He appeared at the doorway with a sheepish look on his face. His years in foster care sometimes made him afraid if he wasn't included in something. No matter how many times I told him that

206

adoption was permanent, he still worried. I used to joke with him that I couldn't get rid of him if I wanted to. But I didn't do that anymore, because he took my hand one day and said, "That's not funny, Mommy. Please don't joke like that anymore. It bothers me." I never did it again.

"Aiden, don't look so sad! This is something *good*! You're going to spend the night with Lily!"

He ran up to me and took my hands. "Really? I get to go to Lily's?" When I smiled and nodded, he said, "Thanks, Mommy!" And then he hugged me.

The three of us walked out to my blue RAV4 in the back. Aiden jumped in the back and buckled himself in without asking to sit shotgun. Bingo jumped in after him. Petra commented on how awesome the car was. I dropped Aiden off at Kasey's without going inside; I waited until Lily opened the door and let him in. Then she slammed the door. She was a handful. It would take me two days to calm Aiden down after their visit, but I had to keep him safe—just in case.

As we drove away, I asked Petra, "Aren't you afraid of being in my house tonight?"

"I told ya, Lorry. I'm used to empty threats. And neither the paint nor the phone call were personal. Neither was the email. They're meant to threaten and intimidate you, not to hurt you."

"What? Are you studying psychology again, Petra?"

She smiled at me. "You know that's my major, Lorry. And by the way, intimidate is from Medieval Latin meaning to frighten, make afraid. He or she just wants to scare you, that's all."

When we pulled up to the house, I was surprised to see Mason's motorcycle already parked there. "Oh, he got here early. He said six."

"He must have gotten out of class earlier than expected," said Petra. She looked around. "But where is he?"

"Maybe he went into the back to play on Aiden's swings," I suggested.

We stepped out of the car and were heading to the front door when it opened and Mason stepped outside. "Welcome home!"

"How did you get into my house, Mason?" I asked.

"Easy," he said, as he moved aside to let us pass. After closing the door, he looked at me. "Lorry, you don't have a deadbolt on your door. And you don't have a dowel inserted in your back sliding glass door. With everything going on, don't you think you ought to be more careful?"

"I thought you were going to be a doctor, not a cop," I said petulantly. "And you still haven't told me how you got into my house."

He reached into his pocket and pulled out a credit card. "With this."

CHAPTER FORTY-FOUR

"HONESTLY, I CAN'T believe you would do that, Mason. I mean, we're friends and all, but—"

Mason put his hand on my shoulder. "Lorry, Petra told me that someone is threatening your life, and you're worried about it. So *I* can't believe you don't have a deadbolt on your door. This is not a smart thing to do. I would have gone to the hardware store and bought one for you and installed it, but they had already closed by the time I found out."

Sighing, I tried to hide my embarrassment. "Thanks, Mason. I appreciate that."

"Anyway, what's done is done, and we'll guard you tonight. No worries. I already ordered the pizza. And when we finish eating, I'm going to slaughter you at chess!"

"Yeah, yeah, right, right. I'm going to go change clothes." I walked toward my bedroom with Bingo following.

"Hey, Lorry! Where's the kid?" Mason called out to me.

When I heard Petra tell him that we dropped Aiden

off, I continued into the bedroom and closed the door. I pulled off my skirt and blouse and put them away. Then I put on a bright, lively blouse with flowers on it and matching slacks. Just in case I got killed tonight, I still had to be stylish. But I decided to forego my heels. For now, at home like this, I could skip the heels and just be comfortable in bare feet. As long as my toenails were nicely polished, I could still be considered stylish. And I liked feeling stylish.

The doorbell rang before I finished dressing, so I knew the pizza had arrived. Unfortunately, I also knew what Mason had ordered: double pepperoni. I liked pepperoni, but double pepperoni usually gave me indigestion. Ah, well. It was Friday, so I had all weekend to recover.

The three of us sat at the kitchen table to eat. Petra and I had two slices each, sharing a third, and Mason ate the rest. Boy, could that kid eat! Mason told us about life at the university, Petra told us about her heavy schedule finishing her last two years of high school and starting her first and second year in college all in one, and I talked about all the incidents surrounding the murder.

"I bet you're glad that jerk is dead though, huh?" asked Mason between bites.

"Shhhh! I'm not supposed to say that to anyone, even if it's what I feel!"

Mason flapped his hand at me, and I was glad he didn't pat my hand, because his was covered with tomato sauce and cheese. "Lorry! We're family! You can tell us anything."

Closing my eyes, I sighed. "Please tell me you're not going to ask me if I did it."

Mason laughed. "Of course not! I *know* you didn't do

210

it. If you had, you wouldn't have killed him in that car you loved so much!"

That made me laugh, too. Whatever reason people had for knowing I didn't do it suited me fine. Billy knew how much I loved my car, too, so I could still be angry at him for taking me into the jail and all. But after the story he told me, I felt more sorry for him than I felt for myself while being in the confines of that small concrete holding cell. Poor Billy.

While Mason stuffed the last of the pizza in his mouth, I cleaned the table. After Mason washed his hands, he retrieved the chess set and set it up on the table. Then he took Petra's hand and looked her in the eyes. "Sweetie, don't worry. I'll beat Lorry in a jiffy, and then we can spend some time together."

"Don't be so sure of that one, Mason ole boy. I'm not distracted like last time we played!"

"You will be. All I have to do is remind you of Eddie's death, the jail cell, the paint on your door, the phone—"

"Okay, you've made your point! But we'll see."

"Forget it, both of you. I have a lot of studying to do yet. Take your time." Petra kissed Mason on the lips and walked into the living room.

Mason made a mistake early in the game. I saw it, and it was a mistake that only someone inexperienced would make. It made me wonder if he was doing it deliberately to let me win. Maybe he thought I was feeling bad enough about being accused of murder and all. He teased me constantly, but he had a good heart, and that is something he would do. So instead of taking advantage of his error, I played around it and ignored it. And Mason didn't make any attempt to fix the mistake. Finally, I decided it was time to take advantage of it, so I moved in that direction and won. Mason looked up like he was surprised. I didn't know what to think.

Mason was putting away the chess set when the doorbell rang. Bingo barked. I heard Petra in the other room call out, "I'll get it."

"Be careful!" Mason shouted.

"Hi, Billy," Petra said.

Billy walked into the room and sniffed the air. "Any pizza left?" Then he looked around. "Where's the kid? In his room?" He turned to go see Aiden.

"Mason ate it all!" said Petra.

"Mason? Again?" He patted Mason's flat stomach. "Where do you put it, Mason?"

"Aiden isn't here, Billy. I dropped him off at Kasey's. You still haven't told me what you found out in San Francisco!"

"Later. I'm starved." He opened my refrigerator. "What do you have in here that I can eat?"

I gently pushed him away from the refrigerator and closed the door. "I'll fix you some eggs and bacon if you tell me what you found out." Petra and Mason just smiled as they watched us going at it.

"Oh, Lorry!" He sat at the table. "All right.

"She was there. But it wasn't her aunt, it was her cousin. Apparently Renee thought an alibi would have more weight if it was an aunt rather than a cousin."

"Maybe the cousin lied completely and Rita wasn't there at all."

Billy shook his head. "Aren't you going to start the eggs? I'm starving here."

"Finish the story, Billy." Mason and Petra chuckled.

"When the aunt slash cousin wasn't home when I arrived, I walked to the neighbors on both sides. One

212

was a retired woman and the other was a woman with young children at home. They both confirmed they had seen Rita when I showed them a picture. Then I went to the cousin's workplace to talk to her. End of story!" He pretended to pound his fists on the table. "Let's eat, woman!" That made Petra and Mason burst out in laughter.

"Okay, thank you," I said as I turned to the refrigerator to remove some bacon and eggs.

While Billy was scarfing down the food and asking for more, Petra piped up, "Lorry, did you tell him about the threatening email?"

Billy dropped his fork on his plate with a loud clacking sound and said, "What?"

While I prepared more eggs, I decided to get back at him for making me wait, so I replied, "I'll tell you when you've finished eating, Billy. Take your time."

CHAPTER FORTY-FIVE

BILLY STOOD UP and with his mouth full, he demanded, "Lorry, what threatening email? When did it come? What did it say?"

I plopped the second helping of eggs and bacon onto his plate. "Finish eating, Billy. It will wait. No worries."

"Don't tell me no worries. I *am* worried! Is that why Aiden isn't here? What did it say?"

Leaning against the refrigerator, I crossed my arms over my chest. And replying with a calm that I didn't feel, I said, "It said, 'Tonight you die, sister!'"

Billy sat down, shoveled more eggs into his mouth, picked up a piece of bacon, stuffed it in, and then stood up again. He rubbed a napkin over his face, crumpled it, and put it on the table. "I need to go to the society to see it now. What's your password?"

"I sent it to my home email. You don't have to go there."

"All right." Billy walked back to my office where I kept my computer. Aiden had one in his room that he seldom used. He preferred books over technology. Smart kid.

The office had a filing cabinet for bills and legal

documents, the wooden desk that the computer sat on, many bookshelves—like every other room in our house —a couple of comfortable chairs, a desk chair that was one of those contraptions with a ball for a seat, and reading lamps by the comfortable chairs.

Billy sat at the desk, turned the computer on, and waited. When the computer started up, he clicked on my email program.

Standing behind him, I said, "It should be one of the last ones."

Billy found the message and tensed up when he read it. "It's a screen print."

"Yeah, I did that so I could send it home."

"You could have just forwarded it home."

"Oh, yeah. I never thought of that."

Billy stood up and held out his hand. "Gimme the key to the society and your password."

I didn't have the key on me, and I don't know what possessed me, but I slapped his hand. "Why?"

"Because I have to see where it came from, and I can't from a screen print. That's why."

"All right. The key is in here." I walked into my bedroom where my purse was, and he followed me right in. Looking up at him, I said, "Can't a girl have any privacy around here?"

"Why? Are you hiding your purse in case I steal all your money?"

"I don't keep money in my purse." I shoved the keys at him. "Here."

"And your password?" He raised his eyebrows at me.

"Petra will give it to you." I walked into the living room with Billy right on my heels. "Petra, tell Billy what my password is."

Petra laughed. "No more Eddie!"

Billy frowned at me. "You never changed it?"

"No, I never changed it!" Billy recognized the password, because he had seen the slip of paper that Petra gave me when I first got the job. "Why should I?"

"Well, you should change it now! If anyone found out about this—" He didn't finish the sentence, he just shook his head. "I'll be back in a few." Stepping toward the door, he stopped when Mason spoke to him.

"Lorry, aren't you forgetting to tell Billy something?" Mason asked.

"You mean that you broke into my house using a credit card?"

Billy turned around quickly. "What's this?"

"She doesn't have a deadbolt on the door, Billy. Someone threatens her life and there's no deadbolt on the front door and no dowel in the back sliding glass door."

Billy shook his head again. "Oh, Lorry." After examining the door and doing more head shaking, he went out, then popped back in again. "Lorry, while I'm gone, you need to arrange to stay somewhere else for the next couple of nights."

"What are you talking about? This is my home. I'm not letting any empty threat"—I winked at Petra—"scare me off!"

"Tonight, we'll all stay here with you. Tomorrow and the next night, you need to find another place to stay. Someone could throw a firebomb in here, and you might not be able to get out of the house safely." He pointed at me. "I'm telling you, you're outa here!" And he stepped out the door and slammed it behind him.

"Mason, why did you do that?"

"Because I care about you, Lorry. I don't want anything to happen to you, and not having a deadbolt in a situation like this is just stupid."

"Are you calling me stupid, Mason?" I asked, with my hands on my hips. "I just killed you at chess." When he blinked at me innocently, I said, "You *did* let me win! You little creep! Do you really think I need your sympathy and pity?"

Mason shrugged, and then he and Petra burst into laughter. They seem to laugh a lot around me. Is it me or is it them? That question haunts me sometimes. And if it's me, then I think that I need to make a change in my life. Then something occurred to me. "Did I hear Billy right? Did he really say '*we'll* all stay here with you'?"

Petra and Mason smiled at me and nodded. I wasn't sure what to do with that information.

CHAPTER FORTY-SIX

WHEN I AWOKE the following morning, everyone had already gone. The night before, when Billy returned, Mason, Petra, and I were watching the end of a movie. Billy got busy installing a deadbolt on the front door and putting a dowel into the track of the sliding glass door. When I asked him how he got those things at that hour on a Friday night, he said that he had connections. He stayed up all night keeping watch. Then he, Mason, and Petra all left at dawn.

Billy had said that the threatening email was sent from an anonymous account, so he couldn't find any information about it. He still felt concerned though. My phone rang. I got up, stretched, and then pulled the phone out of my purse, which was on the chair of my bedroom. Billy rarely used my landline.

"Hello. . . . Yes, Billy, I'm awake. . . . No, I haven't had time yet to call Martha. . . . You don't have to do that. I'm perfectly capable of calling her myself. Stop acting like my father. I can take care of myself. . . . Yes, I promise you that I'll do it right now. . . . Goodbye." As instructed and promised, I called Martha to see if she

218

had room for the next couple of nights. Then I called Kasey's house to talk to Aiden.

"Hello, Lily. Is Aiden there? Thanks. . . . Hi, Sweetie. Are you having a good time? . . . Good. Glad to hear it. Listen, I was wondering if you wanted to stay there tonight and tomorrow night or if you want to come to Grammy and Grampy's with me. . . . Oh, long story. Billy thought it would be a good idea. . . . Yes, um, it does have something to do with the murder. . . . Yes, I'll be fine. So you want to stay at Lily's then? . . . Oh, she does? Tell her I'll call her back later. . . . Sure. Love you, too. Bye."

Kasey wanted to talk to me. And I did not want to talk to her. I didn't ask her if Aiden could stay there another two days because I knew it would be all right. It always was. Lily loved Aiden as much as he loved her. So Kasey wouldn't deny her. But I had no idea what Kasey wanted to talk about. Certainly it wasn't about Aiden's behavior. He couldn't compete with Lily on his worst day. What could it be about then? Whatever it was, I didn't want to hear it right now. If I started on the phone with her, I might not get off for an hour or more, and I wanted to get out of the house, before Billy came over and escorted me out.

After getting dressed, eating breakfast, cleaning up, and packing a bag for my two nights away, I was ready to leave, but my keys weren't in my purse. I searched the house to no avail, and as I was about to call Billy to find out where he had left them, I found them on a table by the door. Locking up with my new deadbolt, I gave the house a last look—just in case someone torched it while I was away—and drove over to Martha's house with Bingo in tow.

The two days and nights passed quickly. Besides Martha and I chitchatting the days and nights away, Martha and Hugo had a couple from England staying at the bed and breakfast, so I enjoyed two breakfasts with them. They were from Essex, and I got to hear all about that, and listen to their wonderful accents. It was fun.

Luckily, I remembered to bring work clothes with me when I went to Martha's, because I woke up late on Monday and didn't have time to stop at home and change clothes. I wore my blue print dress with matching shoes. And I looked fine—even if I did have to say so myself, which I did.

When Bingo and I entered the historical society's building and walked by Petra, she said, "Hey, Lorry. Did anybody burn down your house over the weekend?"

Although I thought she was just trying to be smart, she looked sincere. "I don't know; I came straight from Martha's, but I heard no sirens over the weekend." Rutledge was a small town. If there was a siren, you could hear it just about everywhere.

Sitting down at my desk, I switched on the computer, and while I waited for it to start, I put my purse in the bottom drawer. When the computer came up and I tried to get into my email, I couldn't. I tried once more and then realized what happened. Billy must have changed the password. "Hey, Petra, did Billy tell you what my new password was?"

"No, he didn't tell me."

I was about to call him, when I opened the top drawer of the desk where I kept pens and pencils and miscellaneous small office supplies. Inside lay a business-sized envelope addressed simply *Lorry*. It was still sealed. I opened it with the letter opener, and inside was my new password. Holding the paper in my hand, I just stared at it. What was with that guy, and whatever could this mean? The password, that Billy had apparently come up with himself, was *Hello Billy*. He had changed it from *No More Eddie* to *Hello Billy*. Was I making too much of this? Apparently I was, because he hadn't shown any interest despite what Petra and even Bryan had suggested. I ripped the paper into tiny little pieces and put them in the wastebasket. Shaking my head, I keyed the new password into the computer.

CHAPTER FORTY-SEVEN

AN HOUR AFTER Aiden should have been dropped off at school, Kasey came in with a serious expression on her face. "You didn't call me, Lorry, and I have something important to tell you. Well, *I think* it's important, and I think you should know. And I know that you're probably mad at me for blabbing about that personal stuff, but you know I can't help it, and that I didn't mean anything by it. And maybe this information will make it up to you somehow. I hope so, anyway."

Sighing, I nodded my head. I'd never seen her so serious. But sometimes when Kasey gets started, you can't get her stopped. "Yes, Kasey, I forgive you. What is it?" I had no idea what it was or why it would be important to me; I just wanted to get her out of there so I could have my peace.

"About a month ago, Rita and Renee Croft were in the cafe—without Eddie—even though Eddie usually came with them, but he wasn't with them that day. And Renee was trying to talk Rita into taking out insurance on Eddie. Rita said that she couldn't unless they were married, and she wondered why would she want to, anyway. And Renee said insurance was always important when you loved someone. They went round and round, and before they left, Rita had agreed to see if Eddie would get married, and then she would take out the insurance. Renee told her to be sure not to tell Eddie why she wanted to get married. It meant nothing to me at the time, but after Eddie died, and when I thought about the whole thing, it sounded sneaky and dirty to me.

"Maybe it doesn't mean anything and maybe it does, but I thought I should tell you." She looked at her watch. "Oh, gotta get back! See you!" Kasey slipped out the door and then stuck her head back in. "By the way, I'm sure you'd like to know that Aiden was a perfect gentleman the whole time he was over, and the kids had a blast together! Bye!" And she slipped out the door. All the information that she gave me made me feel guilty that I had avoided talking to her all weekend.

And I sat at my desk completely flabbergasted. I heard the wheels on Petra's chair move across the floor, and then she was there standing next to me.

"I heard that, Lorry! Wow! You need to call Billy now! This is huge!"

I nodded. "Yes, call Billy." My mind was going so fast, I could barely contain it.

"C'mon, Lorry! Call Billy! Or do you want me to?"

Still recovering from the shock of the news, I reached for the phone in a fog, and punched the sheriff's station number. Was it a good thing or a bad thing that I had the number memorized? Probably not good. When they answered, and I asked for Billy, and they said he wasn't there, I knew what I had to do. Naturally, I had to check up on the insurance angle myself.

"Lorry? You okay? You look kind of funny."

Without looking at her, I nodded my head again and stared off into the distance. "Did I tell you that I noticed that she had a ring mark on her wedding ring finger? Now it all makes sense."

"No, you never told me that, but you're right. It does make sense. She gets married, takes out insurance on him, and then kills him. But wait. Rita was out of town. So—"

"It's Renee. She orchestrated everything. Now I have to get proof of the insurance angle."

"That's not your job, Lorry. And it could be dangerous if she discovers you're checking up on that."

Standing up, I said, "Petra, Billy isn't there, and every minute wasted is a minute she's not only getting away with killing Eddie, but she's planning—has probably already planned—another murder. I have to do it!"

Before Petra had a chance to ask what I was talking about, the door opened and a couple walked in. They were dressed in comfortable clothes you might wear on a car trip, and they were smiling. In their fifties, they looked like they were on vacation and were enjoying every minute. Their sense of contentment and delight spilled over and made me forget the gravity of the situation for the moment.

The man peered down the hallway toward the back and said, "Any chance we can get a tour?" He looked around the room. "It's a beautiful old building—well, except the part that's a coffee shop!" He and his wife both laughed, and Petra and I joined them.

"Agreed," I said and pointed toward the back. "Well," I hesitated, knowing it was my job and wishing with all my being at that moment that it wasn't, "it's pretty self-explanatory."

Petra, the darling girl, walked down the hallway in front of them leading the way, beckoning them on with her arm. "I'd be happy to take you on a tour. Follow me. Lorry has business to take care of." She glanced back at me and gave me a dirty look. She didn't think it was a good idea that I do it, but she knew that I would, regardless. I owed her one for this small kindness. Unless of course I was killed for doing this, and then I could blame her for letting me do something so stupid. Whatever.

CHAPTER FORTY-EIGHT

I TOLD BINGO to stay, and he crawled under my desk and gave me a pitiful look. But I needed to do this alone, so I told him I was sorry, and then I slipped out the door before Petra could change her mind.

There was one insurance agent in town, and I knew exactly where his office was. It would have been wiser of them to go to an insurance agent in Coyote Moon, but nobody said the Croft sisters were wise. Walking across the street, I tried to formulate how I would approach the problem. Certainly there were rules governing giving out the details of someone else's life insurance policy, so I had to figure out a way around it.

And I knew who the agent was. His name was Ronald McDonnell, and you can bet he was teased in school for having that name. It was close enough to that other name that kids constantly made fun of him. Not me, of course. Which is why, I'm sure, that all through high school Ronald McDonnell had a crush on me. Although I never did and never would have gone out with him. I wasn't desperate—oh, wait, I was desperate! But not that desperate.

I walked down End Street to the corner of River Road, which was the crummiest, dirtiest street in Rutledge. If it wasn't so hidden and tucked away down there by the river, it would have been reclaimed years ago. Reclaimed. Isn't that the euphemism they use to describe buying your property for less than its worth and then building fancy buildings you couldn't hope to afford? Whatever, they hadn't done it yet.

Ron's small building, about ten feet across and thirty feet long, was freshly painted and looked trim and well-kept compared to the old car parts stores and junk yards that completed the rest of the block. It had an upgrade since Ron had inherited it from his father.

Opening the door and stepping inside with a smile, I was greeted by Ron who jumped up from his chair and gave an exaggerated bow when he saw me. "Lorry Lockharte! So good to see you! It's been ages since I've seen you, dontcha know!"

I had to take a step back to keep him from wrapping his arms around me in a big hug. When he noticed, he sat down to look more dignified and businesslike. Perfect. "Hello, Ron. It's great to see you, too." Sitting down opposite him in the chair by his desk, I smiled my beguiling smile at him. At least I hoped it was beguiling.

"What can I do for you today, Lorry?" he asked, with his eyes sweeping over me. "Business or pleasure?"

I made my smile bigger and even more beguiling, if that was possible, and said, "I was in the neighborhood and thought I'd stop by. Guess I was feeling nostalgic for the old high school days." I shrugged and chuckled and looked above his head as if I was remembering something fantastic. "How can I ever forget that Hail Mary pass you caught in the end zone that won the

227

game! It was awesome!" Bringing my eyes down to his, I nodded. "It was really great!"

A Hail Mary pass, in case you're not a football aficionado, is when the quarterback—that's the guy who throws the football after the guy behind him with his hands on his butt, hands it to him—throws the ball all the way to the end of the football field and hopes that somebody catches it. It's generally only used in desperation when the team is losing and they have no other options. The only reason I know about such garbage is that Eddie was into football and never stopped talking about it. I had to pick up on some of the lingo, didn't I?

"You saw that, did you?" He puffed out his chest. "The bullies didn't make so much fun of me after that, did they? Well, a little they did, but not like before. That was a grand time for me, dontcha know."

The truth was that I had not seen that football game. I hated football back then as much as I hate it now. But after Ron made that nearly impossible catch in the end zone, he was the talk of the school. "You were something, that's for sure." Ron was six and a half feet tall and skinny as a rail back then. He hadn't changed much now, except he was starting to gray around the temples.

Still with his chest puffed out, he said, "Yes, I really was, wasn't I?"

"And do you remember the dance after that, when the guys on the football team poured lemonade all over the coach? He wasn't expecting that, was he?" I wasn't at the dance, either, but I had heard about the stunt afterward.

Ron clapped his hand and fell forward on his desk, laughing. "Those were the greatest of times, dontcha know." Ron liked ending his speech with "dontcha know."

"Oh, they really were. Hey, you know who was in town the other day? My friend Sam Katz! Tall, willowy, black hair and blue eyes. You remember her?"

"Yes, I do. She came, when was it, our last year at Rutledge High?"

I nodded. "Yeah, something like that. You seen any of the old gang around?" Holding my breath, I waited for his answer.

"Oh, yeah! Remember Rita Croft? She just got married and came in here with her sister to get some life insurance for her new hubby. Her sister came with her to help her with picking out a policy. You know her sister, Renee Croft, don't you?" Suddenly, his face lost all its color, and he reached across the desk to pat my hand. "Oh, Lorry, I'm sorry. I forgot about your—"

"It's all right, Ron. It was a long time ago." He was talking about the car accident where my sister died and rumor had it that Renee was driving, although she tenaciously denied it.

"A long time ago, yeah, but some things you don't forget, dontcha know."

My business done, I stood up. "Listen, Ron, it was great seeing you. I heard that you got married."

He pointed to his wedding ring, a plain gold band. "Yeah, yeah! I did! She's a sweet looking girl that I met my first year in college. She's a great wife, dontcha know."

Nodding, I walked to the door. "See ya later, then, Ron. Bye."

He told me exactly what I needed to know without any effort on my part, and he even confirmed about

Renee. Now I had to find Billy, if I could. Where could he have run off to now?

CHAPTER FORTY-NINE

THERE WAS NO need for me to worry about finding Billy. As I walked down End Street toward the historical society, I saw his sheriff's car double parked out in front, with the lights blazing. I was stepping up on the curb when he burst out of the building, ran toward me, and put his hands on my shoulders.

"Are you okay, Lorry? Are you all right?" He looked into my eyes like he really cared about my answer.

It scared me, so I laughed to break the tension and pulled away from him. "Why? Was I limping or something? Musta been one of my high heels." I looked down and checked each heel like maybe it was broken.

He snatched his hands away and put them at his sides. "Oh, no, it was just that I was worried about you. You know, the threat and all. Petra told me—"

Flapping my hand in his direction, I said, "Oh, Billy, it was nothing. I just went over to an old high school chum to get some information. He just happened to be the insurance agent who sold the policy to Rita Croft!"

Billy's eyes got wide, and he opened the door for me. "Come on, go in. Tell me everything."

Bingo met me at the door wagging his tail and acting like I had been gone for days. I petted him briefly, let him lick me on the nose, and told him to go find Rocky. He ran off upstairs.

The couple wanting the tour had already left, so the three of us gathered together at Petra's desk so I could tell them what I found out. They were both disappointed that all I found out was what I suspected all along, plus the confirmation that Renee was the one to get Rita to take out the insurance.

"Lorry, before you left, you said something about another murder. I don't get that," said Petra.

"Ah! Well, if Renee is the one who orchestrated the whole insurance idea, but she wasn't the one to get the money, she has to get the money in some way. Killing her sister would be the logical way. Of course, she could take out insurance on *her*, but that's easy enough to do with or without her knowledge."

Billy nodded. "That makes sense, but there is no way I could prove she was planning that. And killing your own sister? What kind of person would you have to be to do that?"

Petra and I looked at each other because of what Renee had done to *my* sister. Billy must not know about that.

"But your divorce wasn't final before Eddie—" said Petra.

"No, but the insurance agent isn't going to check that. I'm sure a marriage certificate is all you need. They probably went to Vegas or something." In my head I was envisioning an Elvis impersonator performing the ceremony.

"Yeah, Lorry's right. There would be no reason to

check something like that." Billy put his hands in his pockets and looked thoughtful.

"Let me think on it awhile," I said, "because if we don't figure out something quickly, then Rita will be dead right along with Eddie."

"Just don't go doing any stupid risky things." Billy moved toward the door. "And keep me posted."

"You say that like I do risky things all the time," I said. He glared at me. "All right, so sometimes I do risky things. I haven't been hurt yet, have I?"

"I want to keep it that way, Lorry!" And he stepped out the door and closed it behind him. While I watched through the window, he turned off the lights on his patrol car and drove away.

"Lorry, what are you going to do now?" asked Petra.

"I'm going to try and figure out what she's up to. I have no idea how to do that though."

The door opened and two couples walked in. One of them had an infant in arms, and the other couple was carrying a small toddler. I welcomed them inside and showed them the way to the exhibits in the back. Then I sat at my desk and checked my email again. Martha had sent an email saying that she was sending over a couple of short documents that she wanted typed. She had sent the email an hour ago.

"Any documents come for me, Petra?"

"No, not that I know of."

I picked up everything on my desk in case it got shoved under something, but I didn't see anything. I looked around the room and didn't see it on my computer desk, or the filing cabinet, or the fish tank. Ah, the fish tank. While I waited, I could stare at the fish tank and maybe the right idea would come to me. Watching the fish and their gentle movements was like meditation for me. It quieted my mind of the constant chatter. I sank back into my chair and let myself relax.

The problem was that Renee arranged the insurance and then killed Eddie to get the money. But now she had to get the money from Rita's hands into her own, and there was only one way to do that. Kill her. The two primary questions were how and when.

I heard a sound behind me and turned to see a woman with her hand on the doorknob. Beside her was a small boy who looked Aiden's age. He was pulling her hand in the direction of the cafe next door. She allowed him to pull her in that direction, and when she glanced in the window and saw me, she shrugged and followed him. They'd be back. She looked disappointed that she couldn't come in.

When I settled back into watching the fish tank, I heard the door open, and the messenger boy walked in and handed me a manilla envelope. "What took ya so long?"

He turned red and looked down, not willing to look at me. "Oh. My mother called and wanted me to pick something up for her. It took me longer than I thought it would."

"All right. No biggie. Thank you."

The boy nodded and walked out. I wasn't sure if he was embarrassed or lying. My guess was embarrassed. Teenage boys generally didn't like admitting they were doing errands for their mothers.

It made me wonder if Aiden would be like that when he was a teenager. Looking at the clock wondering how soon I'd see him again, I realized how much I missed him! Since we had been together, this was the longest time we had been apart. He called me several times over the weekend, and I called him a couple of times, but talking on the phone and being together was not the same. I really missed him.

CHAPTER FIFTY

THE DOCUMENTS THAT Martha sent over for me to type took only fifteen minutes before I emailed the finished copies off to her. I spent the rest of the morning and the beginning of the afternoon directing people to the exhibits, answering questions about the local area, and taking their money for purchases in the gift shop, although Petra was usually the one who did that.

The most interesting event happened early in the afternoon when a couple who had driven to Rutledge in a jeep wanted information about the jeep road where the old railroad between Sedona and Rutledge used to be. There were still remnants of a train or two at the bottom of the canyon where they had fallen.

"Isn't there a road there now?" asked the man. He was dressed in army camouflage and had a pot gut.

"Yes, it's a jeep road only, though. You know, plenty of ruts and narrow passages."

"Is it safe?" asked the woman. She wore skinny jeans, which she filled out to overflowing, and she wore sandals on her feet. And she looked scared.

"As safe as jeep roads are, I guess," I answered

honestly. "They scare me."

"But people drive there all the time, right?" the man maintained.

I shrugged. "Not sure about all the time, but yes, it is an alternate route from here to Sedona. A slow route."

"Does it have guardrails? Has anybody, you know, gone over the edge?" asked the woman.

"There are no guardrails. It's just an old jeep road," I said.

"Nobody's gone over the edge that we know of," said Petra from the other room. "It's a deep canyon. Maybe someone has and nobody knows about it."

The woman gasped. The man shook his head in defeat.

"I don't think you're helping matters any, Petra," I said.

The man grabbed the woman's hand and pulled her out of the building. I heard them arguing as they walked away. Sighing, I turned my head to look at the fish again, because I recognized that man. He was just like Eddie, and I knew he would get his way. He would drive his jeep on that road, because that is where *he* wanted to go. And he would drive too fast, because he was angry at her for not wanting to go with him. And she would spend two hours in total terror. It made me so glad that I was out of the relationship with Eddie. I wasn't necessarily glad he was dead, but I was glad that I would never have to have anything to do with him again.

Aiden came bounding in about then, and I heard Bingo run down the stairs to meet him. "Bingo! I missed you!" Aiden ran up to me and threw his arms around me. "Mommy! Mommy! I missed you so much."

I hugged him so tight that I don't think he could

breathe. "I missed you, too, Aiden! I love you so much!" Looking at him, he looked fine, although he had his shirt on inside out. "Did you wear your shirt this way all day today?"

Without answering my question, he said, "I love you, too, Mommy!" He squirmed out of my grasp, picked up Bingo, and hugged him. "And I love you, too, Bingo!" Bingo barked and Aiden put him down.

As Aiden and I talked about everything he did at Lily's and what went on in school that day, I noticed out of the corner of my eye Renee, dragging her sister behind her, heading toward the door. Quickly, I jumped up and turned the lock so she couldn't get in. She came in front of the window, narrowed her eyes, and pointed at me. Through the glass, I heard her say, "I'm gonna get you for what you did to Eddie! And sooner than you think!" And silently, she mouthed, "Just like your sister!" Then she spit a big honker on the glass in front of my face and pulled her sister back in the direction of the cafe.

I'm no lip reader, but the "just like your sister" comment was obvious. Plus, as she walked away, Aiden asked, "What did she mean 'just like your sister'?"

I hugged him to me, and said, "Nothing, honey. She didn't mean anything." Standing up, I shook my head. "Now I have to clean up her deposit."

"No, Mommy, wait!" And he ran into the back room. He came back a minute later with a cotton swab and an empty plastic sandwich bag, and he was wearing plastic gloves.

When he started unlocking the front door, I asked, "Aiden, what are you doing?"

He looked at me like I should know better than that. "Getting a DNA sample, of course!" Then he stepped outside, swabbed the cotton swab in the spit on the window, dropped it into the plastic bag, and sealed it. Walking back in the door, he had a big smile on his face. "There ya go, Mommy! Evidence!"

"Who taught you how to do that? Billy?" I wasn't happy with some of the lessons that Billy was teaching my son.

"No, Mommy, but I want to talk to him about it. I learned it on CSI. Lily and I watched it over the weekend. That's how they did it."

That was another reason not to be overly happy about Aiden's trips to Lily's house. Although we had a television, it wasn't connected to cable and didn't even have an antenna. We only used it for movies—and not often for that. Aiden and I agreed that reading was more important. But at Kasey's house, she and John used the television as a babysitter for Lily. And they let her watch anything she wanted, no matter how inappropriate. Too late now.

But Aiden doing that made me realize that I should call Billy, not just to collect the evidence, as Aiden put it, but about what she said to me and the implications of it. I punched in the number on the phone, reached Billy, and gave him a brief rendition of what had happened and what I made of it. He said he'd be right over with the forensics team.

CHAPTER FIFTY-ONE

BEFORE THE FORENSICS team arrived, Aiden, looking rather pleased with himself and carrying around his evidence bag, asked if after Billy left, could we go to the library again. He had finished his latest books and was eager to get more.

"Let's wait and see what time it is, honey."

"Mom," he said with a certain maturity that belied his years, "it only takes five minutes or less. You saw me do it."

Suppressing a laugh, I said, "All right, if that's all it takes, then we can go when they leave. But we have to wait for Billy, because I need to talk to him."

That satisfied Aiden, and he went to sit with Petra with his sealed evidence bag in hand. I heard him explaining to her the importance of sterility in the collection process. That kid will be insufferable when he gets older! I shook my head and smiled to myself, feeling so proud of him.

Billy's forensics team consisted of his two deputies who looked like twelve-year-old boys. Nick and Derek. Nick saluted and smiled at me through the window, but

Derek, the one in the process of collecting the sample, looked unhappy. When I leaned forward to check out the window to the right, the red Mustang, Renee's sister's car, was gone. That was good. Because I didn't want her to have any idea that we were on to her.

The forensics team left, just as Billy walked in through the back hallway, having parked his car in the back. Aiden jumped on him before he got to me, so when he appeared before me, he had Aiden still hanging on around his neck. It surprised me to see Billy out of uniform, which was a rare treat. He looked good in uniform, but he looked just as good without it. He really was an attractive man.

I took a deep breath. "Your forensics boys just left."

"Oh, I probably won't need their sample, anyway. I have this." Billy held up Aiden's evidence bag. "Procured with precision by my little pard here." Aiden beamed, and Billy put him down onto the floor.

"Why are you in your civvies? Short work day, is it?"

"No, rather a long work day is my guess, after what you told me. Tonight could be the night, and I intend to be prepared for it. I'd like to go to your house to check your windows, first, though. You have any problem with that?"

"No, of course not." I opened the bottom drawer to get out my purse and hand Billy my key.

"Ah! No need for that, and he patted his pocket."

I shook my head and put the purse away. "Whatever."

"And what do you think of me taking little pard with me today?" Aiden jumped up and down. "And Bingo, too?"

"Please, Mommy, please. Can I go with Billy?" He looked up at Billy and grinned. "We're going to do some cop stuff, and Billy needs my help."

Sometimes I didn't know if the kid was putting me on or not, but I suspected he was. "I suppose so."

Billy swept Aiden off his feet and picked him up again. "Don't worry! He'll be in good hands! Bingo, too!" And with that, Billy whistled for Bingo and headed for the back door. I heard Bingo's little feet running down the stairs before he, too, jumped in Billy's arms. Although I couldn't see it, I had seen it before, and recognized the feet leaving the ground, the soft grunt of the catch, and Aiden's delightful squeals.

Several minutes after they left, my cell phone rang, and it was from my house. That was curious. "Yes, Billy?" I answered. "What's up? Is something wrong? . . . Oh, hi, Aiden. What's going on, honey? . . . Sure, right here." I picked up pencil and paper and began to scribble. "Yes, got it, got it. Any more? . . . All right! I'll take care of it for you! No worries! . . . I love you, too, son. See you soon. Bye."

He had given me the titles of three books that he wanted from the library. Two fiction and one nonfiction, they were all from the adult section and none of them a book that I would have chosen for him or for myself. But he had his own tastes and his own mind, and I always made sure that none of the books had any sex in them. Although, when it comes time for me to tell him about the birds and the bees, he will probably correct me and tell me details that I don't want to hear. I wasn't looking forward to *that* talk.

After I did a quick cleaning job on the window and washed my hands with soap seventeen times to get the stench of Renee Croft off of them, I strolled down to the library carrying Aiden's list with me.

When I walked in, I saw Brandi behind the counter. "Hi, Brandi!" I looked around. "Where's Catherin today?"

"Oh, she's sick again. Another headache." Today Brandi wore a black blouse and white skirt. Usually, it was the other way around.

"I see you changed your outfit today."

"Yes. I realized that it didn't have to be *white* and black. It could be *black* and white."

"So you're not trying to get a job in the casino, then, huh?"

She laughed. "Oh, nothing like that. It's just that, well," she looked at me as if judging if she could tell me or not, "I've been studying reincarnation lately, and feel like I was a pilgrim in Boston in the early colony years."

"Don't get Aiden started on that. He'll tell me that he used to be Clarence Darrow or somebody like that."

Brandi smiled at me. "Aiden is the one who recommended the books to me!"

We both laughed. "Figures," I said.

"Where is he, anyway? I thought he would have finished those books already."

"He has. He's with Billy on some 'cop business,' as he put it." I handed her his list of books. She knew exactly where they'd be and besides, it would take me twice as long to find them. "Here."

She was back with the books before I would have even had time to look in the computerized card catalog. I knew it was faster and more efficient and all, but I missed the old card catalog.

Brandi checked out the books and handed them to me. "There ya go, Lorry. Tell Aiden that I said hi."

"These don't have any adult, um, situations in them,

do they, Brandi?"

"No. Catherin and I both check for that before we give him any books. He seems to have a knack for choosing books without adult situations. I only had to say no once."

"Which book was that?" I asked.

"*Fifty Shades of Gray!*"

We both laughed, and I walked out with Aiden's books. Wherever could he have heard of that book?

CHAPTER FIFTY-TWO

THE REST OF the afternoon—what was left of it—sped by, and Petra and I both left the office at five o'clock. When I arrived home, it surprised me that I didn't see the sheriff's car or Billy's truck in front of the house. Certainly he would have more sense than to leave Aiden alone. I walked in cautiously and found a note on the kitchen table. It was in Aiden's careful scrawl.

Dear Mommy, Sheriff Billy thought it was best that Bingo and I stay another night with Aunt Kasey, so he is going to drop us off over there. I know that's fine with you, because you'll want us to be safe. And I hope you're safe, too, tonight, but I know that Sheriff Billy will take good care of you. He said to tell you that he'll be over before it gets dark tonight. I love you, Mommy. Aiden

That does make perfect sense, I thought, and I was mad at myself for not having thought of it. Bingo might bark, and who knows what crazy Renee Croft had in mind when she said she was going to get me. It could be anything.

I changed clothes into something comfortable, prepared a salad and some leftovers, and after eating that and cleaning up, I sat down on the couch to read until

Billy got there. He arrived at dusk, so I didn't have to wait long. I knew that I had locked the door—the deadbolt, too—when I came home, so it surprised me when the door opened and Billy walked in like he belonged here. He was dressed like Johnny Cash—all in black. That is, like Johnny Cash except for one thing: he wore a gun belt.

"You're getting awfully familiar with my house," I said sternly.

Billy smiled and shrugged and locked the deadbolt behind him. "I parked my truck a couple of doors down. That won't be a problem, will it?"

"Shouldn't be. You don't want Renee to think I have company? Yeah, probably a good idea."

"And the boys are stationed at her house. They'll let me know if something happens or when she leaves." He reached into his pocket and pulled out his cell phone. "Better put it on vibrate right now before I forget. It would be a bummer if the phone rang and alerted her to what was going on."

"Or scared her away," I put in. "Although, she wouldn't know if it was your cell or my cell."

"Better to have her hear silence so nothing disturbs her from whatever it is she has planned." Billy sat a reasonable distance away from me on the couch.

"Well, part of what she has planned involves killing her sister. What if she does it at her house? Can the boys stop that?"

"There's not enough evidence to get a warrant. If she doesn't do it tonight, then it's possible that we'll get the results on the DNA sample we have. If it matches what came off Eddie, that would probably be enough to get a warrant. But I think whatever is going to happen will go down tonight. I don't think she would have said that and then given you time to prepare for it."

"Agreed. I hated that Aiden had to see that."

"You're okay with Aiden and Bingo going to Kasey's? Sorry I didn't ask first."

"Yes, of course it's fine. I feel ashamed that I didn't think of it myself. But he was gone all weekend, and all I could think about was spending some time with him."

Billy reached over, patted my hand, and left his there longer than he had to. "You're a good mother. You have nothing to feel ashamed about. You missed your kid, and it's not like you didn't have other things—like threats—on your mind."

I gulped and said, "Thank you."

Then Billy's cell phone vibrated and Billy looked at his watch. It wasn't loud, but I could hear it from where I sat, which suddenly felt too close. "Yeah. . . . All right. Thanks."

"Did something happen?" I leaned forward with anticipation. Color me scared.

"No. They are supposed to check in with me every thirty minutes. That was their first check in. All quiet on the western front, as they say."

"Renee lives north of here, but okay. By the way, why are you dressed like Johnny Cash?"

"Oh! Thanks for reminding me! Do you have some black clothes to put on? I don't want her to see any movement in here, and that would help."

"Yeah, sure." I stood up, walked into the bedroom, went through my drawers and closet, and finally came up with some black tights and a black turtleneck blouse. When I put them on I felt too exposed, so I slipped black shorts over the tights. Checking the mirror, I looked, turned around, and looked again. "Not bad for an old broad," I said under my breath.

"What?" said Billy from the other room.

"Do you have supersonic hearing or something? I could barely hear that myself!" I said as I walked back out to the living room.

"No, nothing like that. But in the quiet, I heard something. I have no idea what you said, but I heard a voice coming out of the silence."

"Better you don't know then." I plopped down next to him.

"Oh, did you lock your car?"

"Oops." I winced. "I don't usually lock it, and I keep forgetting. Sorry." I stood up to get my keys.

Billy pulled me back down next to him. "No, keep it unlocked. That's perfect."

"I don't want her to hurt my new car."

"She probably won't do that, but she might do something else. We need it open. That okay?"

"Yeah, I guess. What now?"

"We wait." There was silence for a minute or two and then Billy stood up abruptly. "I forgot! I put locks on all your windows. You want me to show you how they work?"

Shaking my head, I said, "No. Aiden can show me. He probably helped you anyway."

Billy sank down beside me. "Yup, you're right, he did. He's a good kid."

CHAPTER FIFTY-THREE

THERE WERE TWO more all clear calls while we sat there talking about nothing in particular and everything in general. Then Billy turned toward me and said, "Lorry, listen, I wanted to apologize again about how I handled things."

This time, I put my hand on his and patted it. "Billy, you've already explained it and apologized. 'Nuff said. You don't have to mention it again. I'm sorry about what happened to your father and that you didn't get to become a lawyer."

Billy sat up straighter. "What? And miss all the excitement of being a sheriff! You know, sitting next to a beautiful woman and all."

I didn't have time to process this because Billy's cell phone vibrated, and it had only been ten minutes. Before Billy even answered it, he said, "Show time," and stood up. "Got it. You know what to do. Bye." He extended his hand toward me to help me up. "You go to the kitchen window, and I'll watch the front."

"Why the kitchen window?"

"Because you can see if anyone goes to that gate. It's

the only one that isn't locked." Starting to turn away, he turned back. "You didn't lock it when you got home, did you?"

"No, no." I stumbled toward the kitchen, because I was too nervous to walk in a regular manner. This cop-stuff is taxing on the ole nerves! I parked myself by the kitchen window and moved the curtain about a quarter of an inch, too little for her to notice, and just enough for me to get a clear view of anyone walking by.

Billy called quietly from the other room, "She just turned down the street. Stay steady." It was easy to hear him because there was only the breakfast bar between the living room and the kitchen.

I wasn't sure what "stay steady" meant, but I did it, I guess. I stood there looking out the window. All steady like.

"Quiet! She just pulled up out front."

Standing there being quiet and steady, I waited to see if she would walk by where I stood. In the silence of the night, I heard something that sounded like my car door opening and closing. Not my car again, I thought. I just got that car. And it's not even a Taurus. Then I heard another sound like a car door, only farther away. What was going on? She still hadn't walked by.

Then Billy was beside me, whispering in my ear. Before he uttered a sound, though, Renee walked by, with her sister—or somebody's body—slung over her shoulder, and in her other hand, a gas can!

"Stay where you are. I'm slipping out the front."

I barely heard the click of the front door as I high-tailed it to my bedroom sliding glass door. As I lay on the floor in my black outfit, I had a perfect view. Just in case, I slid the dowel that Billy had put there out of the track.

Renee unceremoniously dropped her poor sister on the ground. If she was alive, that would've hurt. Too bad we couldn't have saved her. But at least she landed on the grass and not the cement. Renee stepped away from her to pick up the can of gasoline.

Then I heard Billy's voice rise above the din of cicadas that had just come up. "Drop the can and step away from the body!"

Instead of dropping the can, in one movement Renee picked up the gas can and drenched herself in gasoline. "You can't shoot me now, *Sher*-iff." She said it in a way to taunt him. Reaching into her pocket with the hand not on the gas can, she pulled out a booklet of matches. "You know what I used to do when I was a teenager? I used to practice lighting a match with one hand."

By this time I was standing up, horrified. So when she dropped the can, spilling gasoline in Billy's direction, and held the matchbook out to light it, I was already outside and turning the hose on. She didn't have a chance to light the match, thankfully. The force of the spray knocked the matchbook out of her hand and knocked her over, face first. As she hit the ground, Billy was there putting handcuffs on her. Renee turned up her head to spit on Billy, but he pushed her face back into the ground.

"Police brutality!"

"I'll give you police brutality!" I shouted. "I'll spray this water up your nose." The adrenaline pumped furiously through my body.

I heard Billy say, "Bring the car around, gents." By this time, the water had reached Renee's sister Rita on the ground, and she stirred. Billy noticed and said, "And send for an ambulance, too."

251

CHAPTER FIFTY-FOUR

AS YOU MIGHT well imagine, I didn't get much sleep that night. After staying up for two hours waiting for Billy to call, I finally gave up and went to bed. But it didn't do much good, because all I could do was go over the events of that two minutes in my mind. What would have happened if I hadn't gotten there in time with the hose? What would have happened to Billy? I didn't even want to think about it. But think about it I did, until the sky began to lighten, and then I fell asleep for a brief time before the alarm went off.

After struggling through all my morning routines, minus letting Bingo out and fixing Aiden's breakfast and lunch, I drove into work bleary-eyed. I did manage a quick drive-by of the sheriff's station and didn't see Billy's truck there. But that's how tired I was. Of course it wasn't there, because before I left the house, I saw it still parked two doors down from my house. Billy must have ridden in the patrol car when the deputies arrived.

As much as I hoped the car would be parked in back —or in front, I wasn't particular—of the historical society, it wasn't in either place. As I walked by, I mumbled a good morning to Petra.

"What happened to you?"

"What do you mean?"

"You look horrible. And you're not dressed!"

I looked down and to my amusement—or not—I was barefoot. I had my classic beige suit on—with no shoes. Petra and I both began laughing.

"It was a hard night, Petra." I told her the details that I knew and said I could hardly wait to hear from Billy to find out the rest.

Plodding to my desk—in my bare feet—I turned on the computer. Checking my email first, I thought maybe he would email me. But there was nothing there except some forwards from Petra and an invitation for a chess rematch from Mason.

Settling back into the chair, my head was so cloudy, I could barely remember how to breathe, let alone do anything else. If Martha sent over any documents to be typed, I'd have to tell her that I couldn't do it. I turned my chair and started watching the fish, but when I felt my head fall forward, I decided that wasn't the best idea. What else could I do, besides pull myself up the stairs on my hands and knees and curl up next to Rocky?

Then Billy walked in the front door, dressed exactly as he had been last night, except a little wrinkled. He took me by the hand, pulled me up, and gave me the tightest hug I'd ever had. "Thank you, Lorry! You saved me!" Raising his voice a little, he said, "Petra! Did you hear how Lorry saved me? She saved the day!"

"Yeah, I heard, Billy. Are you going to tell us the rest of the sad tale now?"

"Sure thing! Lorry, come on!"

After he released me, he grabbed my hand and pulled

me into Petra's office. "Hey," he said. "What happened to your shoes?"

"Um," I said.

"Don't ask," said Petra.

Then he told us what happened after he left my house. Billy, the smart one, had one of the deputies in the car with him bring a digital recorder. It wasn't legal in court, but could still come in handy. Billy read Renee her rights, and she immediately confessed everything. Her parents, apparently, had disinherited her for some shenanigans she pulled—which didn't surprise me one bit, either the shenanigans or that her parents had disinherited her— and she thought if she could get her sister's money after conning Rita into including her in her will, she would be fine again. Why her parents allowed her to continue living in their house stumped Billy and me, but they did.

Her plan was to give Rita drugs, haul her over to my house, put a plastic bag full of those drugs in my glove compartment, and then set her sister afire in my backyard. So that's why she had opened and closed my car door last night. Billy had one deputy take that as evidence before he drove away from my house. It was Renee's contention that the real murderer—of both Eddie and her sister—were her parents for cutting her out of the will.

"And get this," Billy continued. "The DNA evidence came in. It *was* her DNA mixed with Eddie's."

"Ha. Always the scum, right up until the end," I said.

"And you'll love this—well, Aiden will love it more. His sample that he took so carefully turned out to be better than the one the deputy took. The deputy's had contamination in it."

"Aiden *will* love that. Don't you go making him into a

cop now, Billy! And by the way, that deputy—the one that took the sample—has sure become a surly son of a gun."

"Derek? Yeah. I know, Town Council wants me to get rid of one of the deputies and he's probably the one. He's made other mistakes, and he's only gotten worse lately." Billy shrugged. "What ya gonna do?"

"Get rid of him?"

"No, he hasn't done anything that bad. I have to forget it for now.

"But concerning Aiden, whatever he decides to do, I'm sure, will be Aiden's decision and Aiden's decision alone."

I smiled. "You're right about that!"

Then Billy took my hand and looked sad. "Listen, during her confession, she also confessed something else. Something about your sister and a car wreck. She said she was driving. I'm sorry, Lorry."

"It was a long time ago, Billy. A long time ago. But I always knew she was lying about who was driving."

Billy let go of my hand, smiled, and looked me straight in the eyes and said, "Lorry, how about I take you out to dinner to celebrate you saving my life and risking your own?"

"Risking my own? I didn't risk my own."

Billy laughed. "You didn't realize that you were close enough that she could have doused you with gasoline, too?"

My brow furrowed. "I hadn't thought about that. I guess she was that close, huh."

"You're so brave, Lorry!" said Petra.

"I'm just glad you didn't have to shoot her. You might have nicked Aiden's swing set, and he would have been none too happy with that."

"Not to mention the blood that might have gotten on it."

"Yeah," I agreed.

"So what do you say? Dinner? With me?" Billy looked at me with a half smile and doubt in his eyes.

Was this a real date, I wondered. I was about to smile and agree when Billy spoke again.

"You, me, and Aiden. How 'bout it? Just say yes."

I tried to sigh without showing that I was sighing, which was a contortion in itself. It wasn't a date. It was just a celebration. But, why not? I might as well say yes, regardless of what it was.

Then Billy added, "You, me, and Aiden. You know. Like a family."

Petra looked at me with raised eyebrows, and I said, "Yes, Billy. Aiden and I would be happy to go to dinner with you."

If you liked this book and feel so inclined, please leave a review on Amazon. Thank you! I appreciate it!

And if you'd like to know when the next Rutledge Historical Society mystery comes out, sign up for the mailing list: http://www.ralstonstorepublishing.com/mysteryL.html

Read the third Rutledge Historical Society mystery, *Kousins Kan't Kill*:

When Lorry Lockharte's cousin, Kasey, is accused of murder, Lorry feels like once again she must work to find the murderer. Did Kasey do it, or is she truly innocent as she claims? Lorry isn't so sure about this one. Not only did Kasey have the opportunity and the motive, but she picked up the murder weapon. Will Lorry find the murderer only to discover that it really is Kasey?

Other books published by Ralston Store Publishing:

Time Travel Sweet Romance
Cowgirls in Time Series by Erica Einhorn
A Chill Wind
Wind Beneath My Wings
Against the Wind
The Healing Wind
Ride Like the Wind
Wind of Change
The Way the Wind Blows

Caregiving
The Journey that Matters by Jodie Lightener

Suspense
Darkness in the Light by J.K. Lincoln

India
Not My Guru by Parvati Hill

Women's Fiction/Reincarnation
Two Lifetimes, One Love by Thea Thaxton

Yoga Books
Bathroom Yoga
Airplane Yoga
Wheelchair Yoga
Essential Yoga on Horseback
Exercises for Therapeutic Riding

Death over Divorce